Dedicated to

*Pop, Mom, Dadu, Amma, Nana, Nani, Kakai, Chotomaa, Adi
and all my lovely friends and respected teachers for making me
what I am today.*

THE ADVENTURES OF THE LEGENDARY QUEEN

Author

OINDRILA CHAKRABORTY

Year 7, Grade 6 Student

Author's YouTube Channel

https://www.youtube.com/playlist?list=PLtNxpzYOlwpPH5kvcNRuKCKK8w2VhgoVA

Mentors

Dr. Manishankar Chakraborty (Father)

Dr. Aasawari Chakraborty (Mother)

notionpress.com

INDIA · SINGAPORE · MALAYSIA

ISBN 979-8-89026-677-4

CONTENTS

PREFACE

• 7 •

Hello! I am Oindrila Chakraborty. I am 11 years old and I study in a British curriculum school. I started writing this story with a forest adventure theme in my mind. However, this slowly turned into a magical adventure with some twists and turns. The writing experience was very fun and interesting, with ideas often popping up out of the blue. As an animal lover, I would love to have my characters live in the forest, go on adventures, pick fruits or go hunting. I have a love for creating unique names and that's where I got my idea for the kingdom names like Ziraria. Honestly speaking, the plot twists were by far the most interesting to create and write, partly because I had to be very careful that the twist made sense. There were a few ups and downs while writing this; overall, it was a big learning experience for me. I learned lots of writing skills. I enjoyed writing this, and I hope you enjoy reading it!

AN INTRODUCTION TO THE THRILLING ADVENTURE

Lysandra goes on a field trip to Mystic Rainforest with her classmates to study the rare creatures that live there. She is so immersed in the animals that she gets separated from her class! Now, she must complete dangerous quests, take on mystical animals, and confront the king of Mystic Forest, King Griffin.

Will she find her way out?

Will her fate keep her safe?

There is only one way to find out: Go with Lysandra on this dangerous quest.

Do her parents keep a deep dark secret from her? Discover that shocking secret about her family and herself. Join her in this awesome adventure starting on the next page… Enjoy the thrill!

CHAPTER 1

MEET ME

Ever since I was a little child, I loved animals. I mean every single one of them. I did not have any favourites growing up. I love animals for what they are, not what they look like. Anyways, I should tell you a bit more about myself. My name is Lysandra Smith. I have long blonde hair, and animals are my first love! I also like soft colours, like baby blue, pastel pink, and most importantly my all-time favourite, light purple (when I mean light, I mean the softest, almost white, I guess, purple). All right, enough about me. We need to get on with the story, we cannot just sit and talk the entire day about my likings. I have had thrilling, bone-chilling, hair-raising adventures. I am lucky to have survived them, and that is why I am here sitting with a group of ghost humans (dead people who came back as ghosts but can touch everything and they are my family) and my dad (who is currently in griffin form), telling this story. Let us move on!

CHAPTER 2

MY ADVENTURES BEGIN HERE!

When I was eighteen years old, my class went on a field trip to the Mystic Forest. We were learning about Mystical Creatures. Some of the animals we were learning about were: Saladillio (Salamander + Armadillo); Porrabbit (Porcupine + Rabbit); Giraffphant (Giraffe + Elephant) and so many more. These are special animals that only live in the Mystic Forest. Unfortunately, I was so immersed in the Saladillio that after some time, the class moved on without me because I was still looking at the Saladillio. After about five minutes of looking at it and jotting notes down in my little purple diary, I realized that I had gotten separated from my class! "Oh no! What am I going to do?" I exclaimed, nervous about what might happen to me now. I wandered about aimlessly, but the more I wandered, the deeper I went into the forest. Eventually, I came across a ghost town. It was so creepy in there! I drifted around the town and found a schoolhouse. When I stepped in, I saw something that made my stomach feel upside down. There were blood splatters everywhere. I immediately dashed to check every single house. I found what I had expected. Yes, you guessed it right. There were blood splatters in every house I had come across. At last, I found a place to rest my shaking legs, but I was wrong. There was something written on the cold, stone wall. It said:

"Whoever you are, if you have the patience to read this, read it. If you can find King Griffin, defeat his army of vicious rats. They will gnaw your eyes out and shred you to pieces. You shall be free to go if you defeat the rats, but if you do not, I am afraid he shall have to keep you as his servant. We are looking for a girl named Lysandra Smith. Lysandra Smith, if you find King Griffin, a grandiose thing awaits you, which may be good or bad. Fate will decide that."

I read this message two or three times. They were looking for me? I did not know what I was thinking, my heart was beating so fast I thought it would burst! I knew for a fact that there were many things we did not know about the Mystic Forest, but I had no idea that it had a King ruling it! Especially a king who is in the form of a griffin! I immediately ran to a building that looked like a hospital. I was shocked to see what had become of all the patients, doctors, nurses, and other people. They were eaten. I ran my hand over dried blood marks, which felt like someone had been dragging their fingers on the wall, creating those marks. They fought for their lives. Even the children it seemed had the same fate. I felt so sorry, but I was going to avenge their deaths by confronting King Griffin and fighting those rats.

At that time, I thought that it was going to be easy. But, oh boy I was wrong! It is not going to be as easy as it sounds. I do not want to give away too much, but I am going to meet my new friends and family in the following chapters, so make sure you keep reading to see how we bond. This is where the real adventure starts. I might interrupt some parts to explain to you whatever needs to be explained at that time. But continuing…

I set off on the long, exciting journey. Soon, I realized that I was going to need food! It was starting to get late, but lucky enough for me, I found some wild berries. I made sure that they were safe to eat. Yes, they were. I gobbled up a lot of berries and then I found a stream. I drank a bit of water, freshened up, and was ready to go. I thought, "That was not a lot of food, and I am still hungry, but at least I found some food to eat and did not entirely starve." But then another problem faced me, it was night-time! "What am I going to do now? I have had food, but now I need shelter to rest for the night!" I cried aloud. I was so nervous!

My teacher told all of us that at night dangerous beasts—which belong to King Griffin—come out to hunt for food, and they especially love to eat humans! They were basically mutated humans which sort of makes them cannibals. I ran around frantically trying to find shelter but to my dismay, I could not find one… Oh well, I would have to camp in one of the houses. I somehow found my way back to the ghost town and searched for shelter there. I chose a house furthest from the entrance just in case the beasts came along. I made my bed (it was comfortable) from the ruins of a bedroom. As soon as I dropped into the bed, I heard huge (when I say huge, I mean it) footsteps. I carefully peeked outside the window and saw the humongous beasts walking around, they were the king's beasts. They were looking for something or SOMEONE. I thought, "Are they looking for me?" I crawled under the bed out of fear. We had studied them in our science class and learned that they do not have good eyesight or smelling skills. They must be assigned to smell, hear, or see something or someone as a target to prey upon. I remembered the message that was written on that rock. I am pretty sure that King Griffin doesn't know how I smell, even if I am his daughter (as he likes to claim) because one, I have never seen him, and two, he has never seen me either. A few seconds later, they barged into another house. They roared so loud that I could hear them clearly. The windows rattled so hard that I was scared it might shatter. I could hear them bellow, "Lysandra Smith, we shall come to get you sooner or later!"

Finally, after 5 minutes or so, the creatures left. I slipped back onto the bed and fell asleep.

CHAPTER 3

THE NEXT DAY

I woke up but did not open my eyes and thought, "That was such a crazy dream!" I was foolish enough to think that I was safely back at the camping site with all my friends. I finally opened my eyes and was shocked to see that it was not a dream but reality! I pinched myself… once… twice. Nope. Real. I sighed and said, "A new day starting now I guess." I kicked up my legs and woke up. I went over to the door to open it and… my eyes met people. But the thing is, they were not people, they were pale and very transparent. I gasped because that is when it hit me. They were ghosts. One of them offered me a bowl of what looked like vegetable soup. It looked very thick, warm, and delicious. I reached out to accept the bowl but then… my arm went THROUGH the bowl AND the person's hand! I frowned at my misfortune of not being able to drink the delicious-looking soup. The group of people understood what was going on and one of them spoke. I must have jumped up a foot in the air, as a young woman with long hair said, "Oh, I forgot about that. Humans will go through whatever ghosts are holding…" She put the bowl down and it immediately became opaque, I picked it up and tasted it. Soon I started feeling better, but I had not realized in my excitement how hungry I was.

So, after consuming the bowl of soup, I asked, "How did you know I was here the whole time?" Two of the little girls hugged me and it felt like being thrown into ICE, freezing water. The adults must have seen my face because they then said, "Kids, break away. You're making her feel cold." One of the toddlers said, "We're sorry, we didn't mean to do it." I smiled at them. I was still trying to wrap my head around and ponder on what just happened. They looked at me and said, "You're not supposed to see us, we are invisible but can choose to make ourselves visible whenever we want to and change into a human whenever we want. We trusted you because we think you are the girl His Highness is looking for."

So, yes. This was a lot of information to process, but then I learned that they have been living here ever since King Griffin's beasts came and killed all the people living in the village. They told me that as soon as I stepped into the village, they could hear my footsteps very well. As they were in close proximity, they could hear me running around. That is why they decided to visit me. At first, they thought, "Who in their right minds would be here in this broken-down, haunted village?" When they got a closer look at me through their invisible presence, they were shocked to see that I was

Lysandra Smith. Next, an elderly woman said, "Hello, dear! Do you want to know why this place is crumbling down? Do you also want to know WHY King Griffin is after you? Also, call me Kim," I nodded slowly, feeling scared and confused at the same time.

She started, "Once, when this village was alive, lively, and people were bustling around, it used to resemble a typical busy day. But, in the evenings, we used to gather around a fire and the older people used to share the myths that they heard. One such myth was: Whoever bears a butterfly mark on their wrist from birth, has the power of nature, and you my dear, have it!" She somehow changed into a human. I exclaimed, "How did you do that?!" Kim replied, "Never mind that." She pulled my sleeve all the way till my forearm looked around and said, "We all have to say a spell together." She pressed my wrist tight with her thumb. I was surprised at this old woman's strength! But I did not show it. Then all the ghosts started chanting in a language I could not understand. The only word I caught was my name. I could not make anything out of it. At last, after five minutes or so, a large butterfly mark started appearing. The moment I was about to open my mouth and ask something, the old lady let go of my wrist and massaged it and said, "I know it must have hurt, but we MUST hold the wrist tight for it to work. I did not make the rules, it is the custom." I said that it was fine and that it did not hurt that much. "Now I am going to teach you all the things that exist and help learn about having nature as a magical element. The fact that you are in control of nature means that you have control over ice, wind, fire, and water. You can create creatures that will follow your lead, but first, you must train to know the intricacies. They are the legendary, Natural Elements," explained Kim. I was still trying to wrap my head around it, but guess what? It was already afternoon! That meant it was time for lunch. All the women started setting things ready like stoves, firewood, and other materials, while the men went out hunting for sport. Half an hour later, the men came back with a couple of lambs. I was impressed; that was quicker than I expected! My thoughts suddenly switched over to my parents. I thought, "I hope my parents are all right and doing well." I wondered what had happened to them. Were they looking for me? Was there a way to send them a letter letting them know that I was all right? I concluded with a negative answer. I had brought my phone with me, but there was no point. No internet connection in the middle of the dense forest! I switched it off for good and now it was just there in my pocket. Oh, I cannot wait to get home after this adventure and meet my friends and family. I snapped out of my trance and went to the outdoor kitchen to help the women. I said, "If I want to get anywhere near defeating the king, I should start learning about my power and skills from tomorrow." Everyone agreed with me. I helped around the tiny outdoor kitchen; we were making lamb stew. One of the elderly women told me to get water in the bowl for her from the nearby stream. I said of course, and now here I am, walking on an absolutely solitary road, a soft breeze whooshing past me, birds chirping to one another and leaves crunching under my battered sneakers. I frowned at them. Oh well, you can always get new shoes any time you want, I suppose. The trees were swaying ever so lightly, the cool breeze on my face. It was perfect. Finally, I reached the stream; it was mesmerizing, frogs, grasshoppers, and so many more marine animals jumping in and out of the water, and basking in the sun. I quickly collected water in the bowl as the elderly woman had requested and made my way back. By the time I returned, the food was made and ready to eat. Sadly, there was no bread to go with the stew. Just as I was about to say it, one of the kids said to their mother, "Wait, Mum, we made some bread a couple of days ago and left it there to dry. Can I get it? It would go very well with the stew." The mom then replied, "Sure, go get it. But make it quick, ok?" She sent out one of the men to go with the little boy just to be safe because they never know what might just be lurking in the bushes; it could be the beasts, waiting to ambush an easy prey. A few minutes later, the boy came back with the bread and shared it equally among everyone. The bread was amazing! It was my favourite, rye bread.

After lunch was over, Kim told me to meet her on the big, empty field. She said that she would teach me the basics of mastering the elements. I took a thirty-minute break after eating lunch and before going over to the field. I was not ready for what was about to happen.

I went over to the field, it was massive! Trees, flowers, and weeds, you name it. Literally, EVERYTHING was in that field. Kim was not here yet, so I sat down in the lush, green-yellow grass and pulled on some weeds as I always did in my house's backyard. I was thinking about leaving when she suddenly appeared out of nowhere. She really gave me a jump scare. Kim looked apologetic, "Sorry, I did not realize that would scare your bones out of your skin. I thought you were expecting me, so, I crept up on you."

"I'm fine, you just startled me. Next time PLEASE tell me before you just appear out of nowhere!" Kim shrugged and said, "OK." Then we started. I found out I had more abilities than Kim thought I would have. She was surprised, and so was I. Later Kim told me, "Lysandra, listen very carefully. The fact that you have more powers than usual is… dangerous and helpful, but it can be destructive as well. VERY destructive. I am not sure. But King Griffin's long-lost daughter is a girl of eighteen, Lysandra Smith is her name. She has long blonde hair, a secret butterfly mark, and more powers than she is supposed to have. It is… YOU! But he will not just believe it that easily. You must prove yourself, and to do that, you have to train a lot. Luckily for you, I used to have powers as well, so I know what to do. We will start training from tomorrow. Get a good night's rest. Also, about the destructive bit…you can burst out with any kind of element—fire, ice, wind—when you are angry, so try to be as calm as possible. Ok?" I nodded and said, "Ok, I will practice long and hard." I then returned to the little hut that I would be staying at over the days that I trained.

CHAPTER 4

TIME TO ESCAPE

After a good night's rest, I was ready to start the training! I freshened up near the stream and was good to go. Breakfast was AMAZING. Berries, bread, and… wild cow milk. Yum! After having an amazing breakfast, I made my way down to the field again. This time Kim was already waiting for me. I wished her good morning and said that I was fresh and ready to start training from today. First, I learned how to summon all the elements one by one. OK, not so bad, good start, I learned that very quickly. Next, I learned to pick up things using the wind and throw them at something. Pretty easy. Success. But then as I was about to learn a new skill, one of King Griffin's beasts came out of nowhere and started attacking me. I quickly did what I could, I picked up a big heavy boulder near me and flung it at the monster. The monster dropped to the ground. I wondered if I had killed it or not. Mm. Probably just passed out. We quickly sneaked out of the field before the beast got back on his feet again. The others were very worried for

Kim and me; they thought something had happened to us because of the loud roar of pain as the monster passed out. Once we got back safely to the camp, everybody was like, "Are you okay?" and "Are you hurt?" We said we were fine and not hurt. Kim proudly explained my actions. Everybody was impressed. The kids listened VERY intently and then bombarded me with loads of questions. After the kids had asked all the questions they could possibly think of, and I answered the best I could, we just chit-chatted for some time. By this time, every ghost was in his/her human form. It was easier for all of them, it was like being reborn, but everybody who had powers lost them. We sat around the campfire, and I told them about my house and family. At one point, my phone fell out of my back pocket, and the eager, young kids picked it up and started throwing it around. I told them, "Stop, you're going to break it!" The kids looked disappointed to have the discovery they just made taken away from them. I said that it was very delicate and could break easily. Then they started firing off questions at me, and as soon as I finished answering one question, another question popped up. It was so chaotic! Finally, after what seemed like a decade, one of the adults told the kids to calm down for a couple of minutes. I do not blame them, if I saw a phone for the first time, I would ask a lot of questions as well. Kim was just teaching me how to turn into a ghost myself. Ever since I got powers, I can shape-shift as well! How exciting! Anyways, as soon as I mastered that (it took a couple of hours because I must focus on being a ghost and not anything else and then when I shifted back, I had to focus on myself) we heard a roar; the same monster that I had knocked over came back, crashing through the trees. "Not again!" I cried. Kim told me to change into my ghost form again, the beasts cannot see a ghost. I quickly changed back into a ghost and soon the whole village was in their ghost form in a matter of a couple of seconds. We quietly floated away from the ghost village towards the stream, or at least we tried to be near it. The stream was being ruined by the beasts, all the trees were destroyed, some completely uprooted. I was really upset to see this, but I kept my emotions in check; the last thing I wanted was for these terrible giants to notice us. We kept floating until we found a nice, comfortable, and quiet spot. We decided to stay in our ghost forms just in case the brutes returned. Soon after, we figured that staying in our ghost form was indeed better because we saw a beautiful, yet scary creature appearing out of the woods. It had the head and body of a lion and the mouth, wings, and talons of an eagle. It was a griffin. Not just any griffin. It was King Griffin. Kim whispered to me, "Do not worry, King Griffin cannot see ghosts as well, so basically, ghosts can see ghosts and everything else, but other animals or humans cannot see ghosts. They cannot even hear us! That is an impressive feature we have. On the negative side, they can feel us though, they cannot touch but feel us. So, that concludes: They cannot see, hear, or touch us but they can feel us. So, we must be incredibly careful while we float around them." I looked at her in surprise because I sure did not know this much! I nodded slowly as I devoured all the information and stored it in my brain because this might be helpful in the future. King Griffin, meanwhile, was just rambling on about something which first did not make any sense, and second, was inaudible. I was feeling extremely nervous because we had started to creep around them and one of the kids accidentally snapped one of the branches when he sat down to take a much-needed break. Everything was tense. The king looked around but found nothing, of course. He went sniffing around, but they also cannot smell us because we are technically just air in the form of humans. We safely got past them and went back to our village. Our village (we called it Village Lysandra now) is already broken down and destroyed by the giants, so Village Lysandra is just a pile of rubble. "When I meet that beast of a king, I am going to make him pay for ruining our Village," I raged aloud. Kim calmed me down with some mint tea. It was good, at least it freshened up my mouth. I calmed down and said, "They know where I am now, we must move tonight. Screw that, we move NOW." Kim clicked her tongue and said, "I see a future queen's order. I see the spirit; everyone does as she says! Quick. Pack the children's toys." And just like that Kim and I started firing jobs at everyone and started helping. We were hustling and bustling here and there, gathering our items, I gathered up the tiny backpack I got before coming on the field trip that led me to this. All my clothes were already dirty, "I'll have to wash them, I guess." I thought to myself. But first, we must find a good place to settle in temporarily.

CHAPTER 5

THE VOICE AND A SHOCKING DISCOVERY

We found a cave as our temporary shelter, and just as we were thinking that the cave wasn't occupied, a grizzly bear came along and tried to attack everyone. I lunged at him in my sabretooth tiger form, he put up a good fight for about six minutes and ran away into the woods, never to be seen again. The kids were extremely tired, so by the time I had finished fighting the bear and making sure there were no other wild and dangerous animals lurking around in the bushes, ready to attack, the cave was already cleaned out and the mattresses laid out, woven blankets, pillows, all laid out and ready to be slept upon. I got my teddy bear out of my backpack and we all had a good night's sleep without any interruptions.

In the morning, just as I woke up, I heard a mysterious voice, and I think everybody heard it because they all stopped dead in their tracks and paused doing whatever they were doing; the children stopped running around and laughing, the adults stopped doing their jobs and looked around to see where the voice was coming from. It was very deep and soft. It said:

Hunting, I am always hunting for you, Lysandra Smith. Wherever you are, I will find you one day. You have not done anything to me, but you are my long-lost daughter! I will take down whoever gets in my way. But you must prove yourself, my real daughter fights with ease, is cunning, smart, and quick. Whoever brainwashed you, Lysandra, will pay.

When the message finished, there was not even a single sound. All I could hear was… silence. Deep, terrified silence. What did he say? "… *my real daughter fights with ease, is cunning, smart, and quick. Whoever brainwashed you, Lysandra, will pay.*" Those are my qualities… And about the brainwashed part? Does that mean… no; that is not possible. Could it mean that my parents brainwashed me? But they love me, we share secrets with each other, surely, they did not keep this from me for… how long did they have me? I had tears in my eyes. I did not know what to think. Soon, everybody was staring at me. I did not know what to do. I felt like a weak girl. Kim whispered, "King Griffin… he sent this message." She came over and gave me a hug. Something I could really use now.

"My parents lied to me, all that time they…" I could not finish my sentence; I was trembling and soon that trembling turned into crying. "I cannot believe my FAKE parents took me away from the real one, no wonder they were always…

distant with me… I feel betrayed. You are the only people who love me now." I said, sobbing into Kim's shoulder. Mary and all the other women came over and gave me a hug and a peck on the cheek. I overheard Sybil (a child's mother) say to Mary, "Poor child, she's only eighteen years old and she has to go through all this." This reminded me, tomorrow was my birthday! I was turning nineteen. I said so to Kim and everyone was excited to hear this. Kim said I could have the day off from training today and tomorrow, but I insisted that I train today to get my mind off things. After a couple of hours of training, I was tired but feeling much better about the betrayal. I could take all my anger out on picking up things and throwing them, transforming into wild animals, and savaging a couple of birds. I know it's weird. I am the person with the legendary nature mark, the long-lost daughter of the king of all animals, and an animal lover and yet I am killing birds, well, at least it's going to keep the bird population in line. I said this to Kim when asked why I am doing this to the poor birds with a casual shrug. The children were pretty upset for me because of the morning's incident, their mothers had instructed them that they were not to upset me again by bringing this topic in front of me. They were also scared of me today, after they saw me taking down those birds with brutality. When I transformed back, my hair had come out of the two braids Kim had made; she said it was too long, but she did not want to cut it as well because the kids LOVE playing with it. It was shining in the sun now. When I was a kid, I used to love playing with Barbies and styling their hair; now I love watching kids play with my hair, styling them into buns, braids, ponytails, and everything they could think of and thought would look good on me. The fact that they loved me and were not afraid to try new things made me smile. Personally, I love it when youngsters are not scared to try new things, fail, then try again and keep trying. I love these kids. They are so sweet! After that incident, they tried to make me feel better; after my training, they made me a flower tiara and we had a tiny role play (which they really liked to do) where the kids crowned me the princess of the forest. For a minute, I was perfectly happy to be just sitting here and relaxing when the same voice came again, with the same message:

Hunting, I am always hunting for you, Lysandra Smith. Wherever you are, I will find you one day. You have not done anything to me but, you are my long-lost daughter! I will take down whoever gets in my way. But you must prove yourself, my real daughter fights with ease, is cunning, smart, and quick. Whoever brainwashed you, Lysandra, will pay.

But this time it added something at the end:

I caught the people who brainwashed you, Lysandra. Wherever you are, tell me how to punish your 'parents,' who took you away from me and injured me very badly when I would not give you up.

I was in complete shock. I said the most brutal thing I could think of. They injured my real father. I sent the message using my elements, the wind. I said, "*Well, dear Father. If you insist, I choose their punishment, please let them hear this as well. Do what they did to you. I do not have an inkling of what they did to you. But DO.IT.BACK. That is their punishment.*" Everybody was shocked because of what I just said. A man, Trevor, said to me, "Well, I didn't know you were such a savage, I always thought of you as the soft kind." I smirked and replied, "Well, many people don't see this side of me, only some of my friends have seen it." I said the last part with a shrug. As soon as I had finished my message, the children started cheering and saying things like, "Yeah! Go Lysandra!" I felt really pleased with myself as well. I spent time together with the kids, telling them more stories until lunchtime, when I first fed the little one and then myself. I still could not get the message out of my head! It was stuck, whenever my mind wandered somewhere else, the thought hit me back, making me decipher it. I kept going back to the same topic, and in the end, it got so annoying I snapped at myself, scaring the kids I was playing with, "Shut it out, Lysandra! Focus on what you are doing!" The adults took the kids away from me and said I just needed some time alone. I got into my cubicle in the pond (which all of us made together over a couple of days), dangling my legs in the cool water, staring at my reflection. Every time I thought of the message, I splashed my face with water to get rid of that thought. Trevor, Kim, Mary, and Sybil all came once to offer me a snack, but I said no as politely as I could despite me snapping at myself to stop. These are the reasons that upset me a lot.

1. I got betrayed by my 'parents.'
2. I got this message, and my birthday is tomorrow.

3. I was really upset when I learned what they did to my real father.
4. I was forced to make a harsh decision.

I calmed myself and with renewed determination, I stood up, freshened up and went out of my cubicle. Everybody was happy to see me again. Mary gave me a big hug. Mary and Kim were so far my favourites, well, everyone was my favourite, but I just liked Mary and Kim more, yes, you get the point. I said so and everybody was elated to hear this. Little did we know, it was dinner time already! The men went out to look for animals (the same setup, half of them go to hunt, the other half stay to protect). Thirty minutes later, they found five plump wild hen and we had chicken stew. The day before yesterday, I had summoned some wheat seeds and used magic to grow them fast so we could make bread, and the bread was ready just in time! All the women (including me, but I am still a girl) made the chicken stew, while I was summoning the herbs that they wanted to marinate the hen meat. The youngsters were styling my hair again this time putting it in a bun. It was a bun on the back, wrapped with a flower crown and some of my hair was dangling down on my face. My new favourite hairstyle was acquired! When asked if I liked it, I said, "I do not like it (disliking voice, frowning. The kids had sad faces) because I love it! (energetic voice, laughing. Children were happy)." I used this trick very often to make people think I did not like it but instead LOVED it. It was funny to see their reactions. When I said, "I don't like it," the mothers looked quite worried because they might start sobbing and a crying child is hard to calm down. Then they looked relieved and started laughing when I said, "Because I love it!" When dinner was made and ready to be consumed, I – of course – helped feed the little ones and then started eating my own dinner, it was delicious! The bread was soft, the stew was warm and the hen meat tender. "You guys cook amazing food!" I said to mostly my bread. Everybody laughed as Kim reached over and swept something off my face and said while laughing, "Guess you really like our cooking if you got it all over your face, huh?"

I replied, giggling, "Yes, I grew up in a rich family so the food was always *fancy* (I emphasized it a LOT) and not as half as good and as simple as this food is!" I wiped my face with the back of my hand. After dinner, we all did our usual night routine, tucking in the children, weaving tendrils of water and fire; after they were fast asleep, talking to the adults then finally falling asleep myself. Before my eyes dropped and I fell into the eternal world of dreams, Kim, Mary, and Sybil came to me, and each gave me a peck on the cheek. I smiled drowsily and fell asleep.

CHAPTER 6

MY BIRTHDAY!

Another morning! What date was yesterday? 13th of January. Nothing special today, is it? Oh well, should get up and get going. The chores are not going to finish themselves (I wish they did, that would have been nice). I sat up and stretched and got a jump scare because everyone said, "Happy Birthday, Lysandra!" AT THE SAME TIME. The first thing in the morning you get is a jump scare. But it was sweet of them, they even served me breakfast in the bed. My breakfast was bread and some of the leftover chicken stew, and what was this? It looked like bread, but it was… softer… bigger… very sticky and looked sweet. Kim saw me looking at it with curiosity, nudged me and said, "Go on try it, it is our traditional village sweet. Thanks to your amazing wheat production, we could make this. We found leftover herbs from yesterday so we decided to use that, Trevor and Josh found some sugarcane, so we could make it sweet." I took a big bite of it and chewed, everyone looked hopeful when

Josh said, "Well? How is it, Lysandra? Eating this for the first time? Oh, of course, you are eating it for the first time. Sorry, I got confused. Anyways, we call this the Phoenix Bread." I slowly said, "It's… AMAZING, best dessert ever!" Soon a voice floated through the air:

"Happy birthday, cupcake. I performed the punishment you wanted me to, and they are looking pretty battered right now. Hope you have a good day, Lysandra."

I replied: *"Thanks, Dad, appreciate it. Aw, I wanted to see the people who tore me away from you."*

After replying, I finished my breakfast and said, "I'm ready for training now, Kim!" But before I could get the whole sentence out of my mouth, she interrupted me and said, "Oh no, young lady, we are not doing any training today. It is your day off." I pouted and said, "There's nothing else to do here, though." I should not have said that because Kim then went off rattling a list of things I could do. Like:

1. Play with the kids.
2. Grow more things in the field.
3. Chill out in the pond.
4. Train more fishes.

and so many more…

When she finished the list, I said to her, "You always have an answer for every question." She said, proudly, "Of course, I do, dear. I am an old and wise person." At this, every elderly person laughed. Mary then said after the laughter subsided, "Looks like King Griffin is going to send you messages very often now, right?"

I laughed at that. Anyways, I know the last activity sounds weird, but I like to do it. Train fishes to swim around and create mesmerizing shows, leaping in and out of the water in a pattern or parallel movements. So, I got up, went over to the pond and my cubicle, brushed my hair and teeth, and took a long bath. I warmed up the water for everyone using the fire element. We even have a kiddie pool for the kids. We just had to shovel some dirt in and set it at the bottom to make it shallow. Easy. Really simple. Straightforward. When I was done taking a shower, I wore the freshly washed clothes that Mary very kindly washed for me. When I got out of my cubicle, I was as fresh as a daisy, looking brighter than the sun, and energetic because, like, you do not turn nineteen every day, do you? You only turn nineteen once in your lifetime. I walked into the camp where everyone was eating breakfast. I helped feed the youngsters so that the mothers could eat. I did not have to worry about that because they gave me an amazing breakfast in bed. I asked them about the Phoenix Bread. How it was created, like how did it come into existence? They said that one hundred years ago, there used to be a very curious child in their village, who loved to cook and make new, weird recipes. One day, he was playing around with the bread that he baked using his mom's help, adding ingredients to it like herbs (mint) and tasting it. The bread was not sweet, so he added some sugarcane juice and then tasted it, he immediately liked it and made everyone try it. They named it Phoenix Bread because his favourite mystical animal was a Phoenix. Ever since that day, this had been our traditional sweet. This was the most heart-warming story, about a young boy who liked to cook and try out new things. I said so, then Sybil replied, "Well, you might be a famous person in our village for a hundred generations or even more if the village doesn't crumble down, Lysandra Smith, the long-lost daughter of King Griffin, saved our village…" And just like that she trailed off and looked around; everyone applauded. I went up to her, hugged her and said while laughing, "You certainly do have a wild imagination, Sybil." She looked proud to hear that. Then they asked me about my other favourite sweets, I said, "Well, I do like pudding, strawberry tarts, ice cream, and treacle." They looked very confused, I do not blame them, because they never heard of these strange sweets. But then I added, "But my new favourite sweet is Phoenix Bread." As I was saying this, I transformed into a Phoenix. I soared high above the cave and camp, using this as an excuse to search for any dangers. Good, no danger. Just as I was about to say this aloud, I heard loud stomping. I immediately swooped down, and tried to say, "Guys, turn into ghosts, there is something coming this way!" They started to laugh because I was a wide-eyed, flustered and anxious Phoenix trying to speak while moving her wings around. I forgot that I couldn't speak in Phoenix form yet, but I could speak in every other form. I quickly changed into a human and told them what was happening. They looked shocked and worried; we all changed into ghosts and floated away. We packed up our things to make it look like we never set up camp there. After packing, I did a final sweep using the wind element across the cave just to make sure there was nothing left. We had to escape again. I flew ahead to see what was going on, and I saw King Griffin himself, standing there, majestically. My heart started beating faster, and it said, no, I cannot face him yet. I do not know how to face him. I do not know enough about how to control the elements existing between us and them. Kim asked me, "Are you sure, you don't want to face him now?" I shrugged and said, "I don't know. I don't want to, but I want to at the same time, I am puzzled." In the end, I decided to show myself to my father. I wanted him to know that I was all right, I was doing well. Just as I was about to do that, King Griffin said, sniffing the air, "I smell my daughter." Mary replied to that, "We completely forgot, you and the king have a special bond which means, no matter what form you are in, he could always sniff you out… But how did he not smell you the first time? Wait… he looked in your direction but didn't say anything, one of his tests… slyness, yes! He wanted to test you out. Whether you would make a sound or keep still. It's that simple!" I replied, "I'm still going out there and showing myself." I walked out of our hideout and revealed myself. His beasts were about to lunge at me, but luckily, the king held up a humongous paw and said in a deep, gruff voice, "Stop. Are you Lysandra Smith (I gave a small, cautious nod)? If so, I want to evaluate if you know this legendary song." He started humming a tune which I could vaguely remember, and a few seconds later, I was humming it myself; swirls of wind, water, fire and ice were surrounding me. I rose majestically and was floating in mid-air with nothing underneath me to support my feet.

Suddenly, all the elements that were surrounding me, plunged inside me. The world went dark for a moment until a blinding white light came from somewhere and I dropped onto the ground on my feet. Everyone, including my dad, gasped when they saw something about me. When I looked down to see myself, I was shocked to see that I changed completely! My golden hair had turned silver (not the ageing white). I was wearing all white with gold embroidery. My eyes were mismatched (how did I know it? I looked at my reflection I created using my waterpower because everyone was looking at my face, trying to make out what happened to my eyes); one was blue, calm, like water and the other was green, quick and agile like a snake. I had a sword in one hand, the hilt had a big garnet, my birthstone, and my other hand had a tangle of fire, water, wind, ice and earth. I was a warrior princess. Oh My Goodness, I could not believe it! Everybody was just staring at me. My father came over to me, got on his hind legs and placed his big, giant paws on both of my shoulders. Many people would have staggered under the weight of his paws, but I did not move an inch. He stared at me, and I kept eye contact. He finally broke the very awkward silence by saying, "You really are my daughter, you know the legendary tune. But you are overpowered, this is an once-in-a-lifetime moment, seeing one's own daughter turning into someone mystical. Do you know who you turned into?" I nodded and said, "Yeah, a warrior princess. I know I've read WAY too many stories about them." My dad took a deep breath and told me, "Lysandra, here is the thing about you, your real name is not Lysandra but Celeste. Let's show your 'parents' and see how they react, ok?" I replied with an ok, sure why not. When I asked him what that meant, he told me that it was best if I know later. After that tiny conversation between my father and me, the others did the most surprising thing, they revealed themselves. The king got a jump scare and looked terrified. He slowly stammered, "H-How a-are you s-s-still alive? I-I thought m-my beasts accidentally k-killed y-y-your v-v-village?" They casually replied to him, "We came back as human ghosts, our village had an enchantment for our generation, your majesty." King Griffin, after recovering from his shock, bellowed (like, it was so loud, I thought my ears might stop working), "Why are you here, and if you know my daughter, how do you know her?" I said to my dad as soothingly as I could, "Dad, take a chill pill. They are the ones who taught me about my powers, they kept me safe, they fed me, and they let me stay with them." At this, he stopped raging and said, "Oh thank you for taking care of her! I am so sorry for what the beasts did to your village. They must have gotten confused; they are a bit dumb. I sent them to ransack our enemy town's village, but I suppose yours comes in the way, so they thought that was the village I ordered them to destroy into smithereens." Everyone said that it was fine and that we found a cosy shelter in a cave. King Griffin then asked all of us to come and live with him in the castle. I could train there, and when I was finally ready, I could face his army of dangerous rats. Honestly, I am horrified of rats, but I guess defeating them will be one of my biggest achievements. The ghosts just floated a few inches from the group while I transformed into a Pegasus. My head is very shiny with long silver hair like a unicorn, but without the horn and with wings. It was such a good feeling, soaring high above with my dad. I suddenly asked my dad, "Dad, what did you do to my fake parents?" The king laughed and said, "You'll see when we get there, it's hard to explain." We flew for a couple of miles. I kept transforming into a ghost, beast, and Pegasus, often also going in a sparrow form so I could sit on my dad's back; transforming is very tiring. I kept wondering, can my dad also turn into a human? When asked, he just shrugged and said that I must wait to know the answer. We finally reached our destination, I was back in Pegasus form and whispered (I learned how to speak in animal form, but I am having trouble doing the same in the Phoenix form), "Ziraria Kingdom… It has been so long; I still vaguely remember this wonderland." My father only smiled at me as we landed in the courtyard of the palace. A guard greeted us, "Good morning, King Lunarquills. Do you want me to let all these people in?" My father nodded. Soon as the guard saw me (I transformed back into my human form, which was now the warrior princess), he bowed down, "Good morning, Princess Celeste. The day has finally come where we can all meet you. An honour." I smiled and curtsied at him. As everybody filed in, I hugged everyone in my excitement and told Sybil, "Oh my god! I cannot believe I revealed myself to him! Phew! That was nerve-racking!" Sybil smiled and replied, "Good job, sweetie. But I must admit, your latest look is cute and looks exceptionally good on you." I said thanks and that I really appreciate it. I must've jumped a foot when I felt a hand on my shoulder. I spun around and was shocked to see a tall man with silver hair like mine. He looked about 2 or 3 years older than me, so I asked him, "Uh, hi, can I help you?" The man laughed and said, "I am Louie, your dad, Lysandra." I looked at him with confusion and said, "Huh, Dad! What is going on? When you are a griffin, you are addressed to as either King Griffin or King Lunarquills and when you are human, you are called Louie? I do not get anything!" He just smiled and ruffled my hair. We all went inside the castle, and it was the MOST beautiful and majestic castle I have ever seen. "I vaguely also remember running to and fro the courtyard and the castle…" I recollected from my thoughts. "Can I see my fake parents now?" I continued. My father nodded and led me into a room. It was a spacious room, with a standard-sized bed. There were two people in the centre. They immediately looked up and said coldly, "Who is this girl in our room? Take her out of here." Louie responded with pure venom in his eyes, "Is this a way to talk to your daughter and the princess?" They replied, "Daughter? You are absolutely nuts; our daughter has golden hair, not silver." I came back at them savagely, "How can you not recognize your own daughter? How did you not realise that by looking at my walking style and my other characteristics? Yes, right, you cannot because you are not my real parents. How did King Griffin (a nod and a smile towards his direction) recognize me after nineteen years? I bet you do not even remember my birthday." My mom's eyes softened a bit as they said, "Sweetie, that's not true. We all know that your birthday was yesterday—" I cut my mom off and said, "No, that is not right, my birthday is TODAY! And do you know who took care of me all this time? These people, they were the sweetest and the kindest people, hugging me when I found out that YOU brainwashed me into thinking that Louie was not my dad. I still cannot believe that you had the audacity to do this to me."

"But Lysandra..." tried my mom.

My dad cut her off with a cold look and said, "Lysandra? Lysandra? She is not Lysandra. She is Celeste Halo, and I am Louie Halo. Yes, I called her Lysandra to test you. She is my actual daughter; she revealed her true form. And the people who took care of her? They care for her more than you do!"

"Those peasants? How dare they go near my daughter?" With that, my 'mom' got up from her chair, went to the nearest person (who was a little toddler) and slapped him right across the face. He immediately started crying. I ran over, hugged him and tried to comfort him when my 'mom' asked me, "Why are you hugging this child? They are all peasants..." Before she could continue, I glared at her and snapped, "Why do you care whom I hug? You cannot control my life. Well, you used to, but now you cannot anymore!" I snarled at her with such intensity that everyone around me backed off. I suppose I have been spending too much time as a feline. I could feel my eyes blazing. Suddenly, my dad said, "Whoa, whoa, she is ANGRY, her eyes just flashed red!

Do not provoke her anymore, I do not want to know her dangerous side." Oh well! I suppose I spend too much time in my lioness form and my phoenix form. But still, if they lay a finger on my new family, they are going to regret being born. I noted that to myself and said so to the Strangers (I am just going to refer to them as Strangers now) who were extremely nervous once they saw that I was serious. I spun around and left the room. When I was out of that room, I let out a long sigh, I really had wanted to say this to them. When Kim and Mary came out, I at once burst into tears and sobbed into Kim's shoulder while Mary patted my shoulder and tried to hush me. When I was done crying, I looked up and said, "You are the best, do not listen to my fake mom, you are not peasants, you have the kindest hearts in the entire world! I am also sorry for what she did to that poor boy..." Mary cut me off and said, "Family don't apologize over such a small matter. Not going to lie, she looked very weak when she slapped him. He probably just started crying because he doesn't like being touched by strangers." I laughed at that, and everyone started filing out. I could hear the Strangers still shouting inside, "You'll pay for letting her know what we did to her." I poked my head inside and yelled back, "Well, this is what you get for TORTURING my father. I sent a spark of fire in the middle of the room that would attack them every time they thought ANYTHING bad about me, my dad, or my ghost friends.

My dad kept apologizing repeatedly for unknowingly destroying their village. He started talking to them increasingly as every day passed by. He sometimes came over to watch me train with Kim and often help me tie my hair in a bun if the kids let him. Because they love my silver hair and they still loved making my hair. I always ask them to make buns when I train. So, today I was training with fire. You know, how to cleanse a wide area and how to burn something from INSIDE. I used a dummy to burn out all the insides of it (it was filled with cotton). I was getting better and better each day. I put in extra effort today because my father was watching. Every evening, he asked Kim about my progress, and she always said I did well, but today he wanted to see me train. Even he said I am making excellent progress! That was a compliment! After training, I always pop into the Strangers' room to refresh and recharge the spark of fire. Everyone was impressed with the spark I sent in. My room was so big! I coloured it with my most favourite colour, the lightest purple that I could summon using my power. I decorated it with lots of tiny trinkets my dad gave me. I asked my father where my mother was and at once his face fell. Then he told me: "I did not know you would ask me this early, I thought you would take some time to get familiarized to your surroundings. Anyways, here is the story: I and your mom were friends with your fake parents. When we had you, they thought we didn't deserve you because we weren't sure if you had powers and they thought we might abuse you if you didn't have powers, which was impossible because we could never hurt you. So, when they STOLE you from us, they made us watch as they changed your appearance in a way that only if you sing or hum the legendary tune, it will wear off. Second, they made a potion and made you drink it with your milk, and it took a couple of days to brainwash you. We did not give you up easily, so they injured both of us. At last, your mom declared war. She fought very bravely, she was a warrior queen, but they did something very unfair. They both teamed up on her, but she changed into a ghost leopard and fought like crazy, but it was two against one and... she lost. They tied me to a tree and made me watch her fall as she fought for YOU. That is why I was so happy to see you, and angry when I did not know about the village people. I did not want you to be taken away from me that easily again." Tears streamed down my face as I was listening to the story. They killed MY mom. I want to avenge her death no matter what. But first, I just needed to overpower them. Be stronger than them. My father must have seen the determination in my eyes and my face because he then said, "Calm down, train as hard you can. If you declare war, I want you to win it. I cannot bear my own daughter to have the same fate as my wife, and I am incapable of doing anything. I cannot bear that!" I soothed him and said, I would win no matter what.

CHAPTER 7

AVENGING MY MOTHER...

I trained harder than I ever had... my dad gave me my mother's favourite scarf to remind me what my mission/ goal was. I was going to fight for her. Finish what she started. It did not matter to me if I lost my own life to do it. I kept training for long hours. Even after Kim had already gone upstairs, I revised what I learned so far and all the moves the royal guards taught me along with the form of the animal it would go well with. Everyone was incredibly pleased with me. All my ghost-human family also said that they were skilled fighters, and they would assist me in the fight. But then I said it was my war, and I would do it all alone to avenge my mother's death. They tried to argue but then gave in because I had already made up my mind. The Strangers did not know how much I was training, I did not give it away too, and I wanted them to think they had an advantage over me when the time came. But first, I forgot that I still had that army of vicious rats to fight. Sigh! I have a lot of training to do. But, if everything is worth it, I am up for it. I slept well, to recharge my powers. I leave the fire spark at night alone and in the morning, recharge it; so far, they have had a few burns here and there. Good, they were not thinking anything bad about any of us. Especially my family. Yes, I consider the ghost humans my family too because they saved my life. If they had not found me that day, I would have been dead by now. There was no way my normal and defenceless self could survive all alone in the wild. So, I am incredibly grateful to them.

Today, however, my dad insisted on me taking a day off. I only took it because I wanted to give Kim a break; you know, she is elderly, so I wanted to make sure she was all right first. My dad then took me to a huge pool where one of the guards said, "Good morning, King Louie. Good day to you, Princess Celeste." I smiled and said, "Good day to you as well." He looked happy when I said that. I nudged my dad and said, "Come on, greet the guard. They stand here the whole day, taking care." He mumbled a good morning. Better. Way better. There was a majestic pool in front of us. I asked, "What are we doing here, Dad? Are we going to swim today?" He replied with a yep and a, get into your swimsuit, you will find it in cubicle number eighteen. As I went into the changing area, I already saw my other family members (the village people, they are part of the Halo family now). I was satisfied; everyone was included in today's activity. I quickly changed; my swimming suit was so cute! It was like a full-sleeved overall with kittens cuddling each other! I loved it! After ten minutes, I was done changing. I did not bother tying my hair. The good thing was that I knew how to swim! I sat in the kiddie pool for about fifteen minutes, just soaking my feet and looking after the children. We took turns to watch over them like a big happy family. When I got into the pool, I just floated around, my silver hair all around me. When it was my dad's turn to watch the kids, I was pleased to see him interacting with the children, making funny faces, and doing funny things in the water. A smile tugged at my lips at this sight. Sybil and another woman (Primrose) with her daughter Camille swam over to me. I love that the mother was named after a flower and the daughter's name meant 'perfect.' I created flowers for both (both of their favourite flowers were primrose and daisies). I created a beautiful and fresh bouquet for them. "I love it!" that is what Camille said. She had a soft voice, like me, which she could change to make it cold whenever she wanted. We were similar in a lot of ways. We both turned nineteen on the same day, we both love flowers and have soft voices, we were both lovers of soft and pastel colours, and so much more. We all spent time together in the pool and enjoyed ourselves the entire day. At one point, I dried myself with the fire element and went up to recharge my spark of fire. I went back down again and heard Sybil screaming. I immediately used my wind to make me run faster and saw that a ginormous snake had somehow made it up and into the kiddie pool. The kids cowered in the corner as the snake hissed and steadily made his way towards fresh and easy prey. I immediately changed into a griffin, picked up the snake, and flung it across the kingdom. My dad came over and thumped me on the back and ruffled my hair once I had changed back. I got in the pool again. This time in the shallow end so I could just float. My hair was already dripping wet. Our dinner was so good today! We had roasted chicken and lamb stew with soft fluffy bread. Kim even taught all the cooks how to make Phoenix Bread. I suddenly started feeling sick, which often happens when I sense danger coming closer. I excused myself, got up from the table, and walked around the courtyard.

Suddenly, a beast launched itself at me, but before it landed its horrifying claws on me, I swept away saying, "Watch it! I am Celeste Halo! I knew your eyesight was bad, but I did not know it was this bad that you cannot even recognize your princess!" The beast looked bashful and said, "I am sorry, Princess Celeste. I did not mean to do it. We have a very selective vision, all I saw was a person walking in the courtyard, I thought someone was trying to enter the castle. I promise this will not happen again." He kept apologizing repeatedly. I held up a hand and stopped him. I continued my walk in the courtyard. Suddenly, I heard another scream, this time from... Camille and Primrose! It was from somewhere near the garden! The poor things, they did not know how to fight, yet! I sprinted down the yard and was just in time to see the Strangers cornering the poor girl and woman. I yelled at them, "Hey! Do not pick on the helpless people, pick me instead!" They turned around and were shocked to see me. I gathered my fire and... it was a blue fire. Blue fire bathed my face, which was coated in disgust and coldness because I did not think they would pick on two innocent, defenceless people! I watched them run away in fear with their tails between their legs (they did not have tails, just imagination). My eyes followed them all the way. I finally let go of my blue fire and my face softened. I asked them, "What are you doing so late in the garden?" They replied, "Um, we just wanted to make you a bouquet, for giving us one at the pool today." I said with a hint of annoyance, which I somehow controlled, "You could have done this tomorrow, you know you worried me to death. I do not want anything happening to you." Camille soothed me saying, "It is all right, we promise we will not do this again. Come on, Mom. We are going to bed, we have had enough today. Let us stop for the day." Primrose agreed and I walked them to their rooms even though they insisted it was not necessary. After seeing that, I went over to the Strangers' room and looked over sternly and said, "What do you think you were doing to those innocent people, huh?" They stammered, "W-What d-do y-y-you m-m-mean? We did not do anything!" I snapped at them with all my reserved anger, "DO NOT TRY TO ACT INNOCENT. I KNOW WHAT YOU DID! Did you think I was not going to notice you? I could see you and hear you from a mile away. Even though I was angry, I still focus on my surroundings. I am not as dumb and weak as you think I am or was. I am stronger. If I see you do that again, I will not hesitate to use this." I pulled out my sword at that and put that thing under their chins and looked at them with venom in my eyes. My fake mom started trembling and my dad said, smirking, "You think you can beat me, little girl? Well, good luck taking me on." I stormed away from their room, I needed to get their smell of evil intentions out of my nose. When I got to the garden, I took a deep breath and out. Hours later, I retired to my bedroom and slept… having occasional nightmares… I am surely going punish those two for making me suffer like this… then I fell asleep.

The next day

The next morning, I had dark circles under my eyes because I could not sleep well last night after the incident with the Strangers, and lots of nightmares. Everybody was very worried about me because I was quieter than usual at breakfast. They bombarded me with lots of questions. After one hundred or so questions, I finally lost it. I snapped at the breakfast table and slapped my palms on the table, pushed back my chair, and went to the garden. I grew a random tree, uprooted that tree, set it on fire, and used the wind to throw it away and pick it up again and throw it again then burned it into ash then blew it away into thin air. That felt good, but I was still angry. I decided to repeat the process repeatedly until I felt calm. It took about eight tries before I was calm again. I just sat down on the ground and started growing flowers. I sighed; I should not have snapped at everyone… I felt bad… It was all the Strangers' fault. How dare they make me so angry and snap at my own family? They were also going to pay. I took a deep breath in and out and went in to face them and apologize. I went into the dining hall and said, "I am sorry, I did not want to snap at you earlier, I just… lost it. Something happened yesterday, and I was stressed, you were asking a lot of questions, so I got mad and snapped." Primrose came over and hugged me while saying, gently, "I think I might know why you were so mad." Yes. She did, it happened right in front of her. Well, she did not hear the conversation we had which made me mad. "We're sorry to ask you so many questions without knowing what you've been through." I smiled and said it was fine, then went up to my room and just sat there, playing, and rearranging the small trinkets, books, and stuffed teddy bears. I got up and went to the Strangers' room, and poked my head inside. My fake dad smirked at me and was about to say something when I sent a huge wave of water into their room, drenching them, then I sent in a more powerful spark of fire, which would cause more burns than the last one. But there are more levels, if this does not work, a more intense one is coming up, and I have been practising. I said so, and they just laughed. I asked them, "Do you want to be drenched again? Because this fire is not going to dry you up. It will make you worse. If you want that, you can tell me now, and I shall be more than happy to have the honours to carry the action out." My 'mom' said. "Oh, please don't do this as it is my favourite dress!" Same old personality, caring more about her dresses than anything else in the universe. I still do not understand, what did he say to make me so annoyed? He just said, *"You think you can beat me, little girl? Well, good luck taking me on."* What snapped inside me when he said that? I do not have an inkling of what happened, it reminded me about my biological mom, how they murdered her in front of my dad, watching helplessly. The trauma must have been very harsh on him. His child was stolen, and his wife was murdered right in front of him, that was enough to break a person completely. But he is still strong, and I respect that. Suddenly, with no warning whatsoever, I sent in a bang of ice, which curled like a snake and hissed at them. It said, "You dare hurt anyone, you'll see what I'll do to you in one night." He requested I let him stay in their room, and I said sure. This… ice serpent-dragon was going to teach them a lesson that was necessary for them to learn. I went out of the room and tried to find Kim. I wanted to tell her about the encounter and train as well so that I could defeat the Strangers. After wandering around for some time, I found her sitting beneath a tree, absorbed in a book. I went up to her and asked, "What are you reading? It looks interesting." Kim looked up, smiled, and said, "I am reading a story about a girl who met a unicorn in the middle of the forest and turned out to be the Unicorn Queen, it's pretty cool." I grinned and said, "Can we train now? I want to learn new tricks. Please!" She began to say no but I made my big and cute puppy eyes until she gave in. I showed her all my skills so far and all the moves the guards had taught me along with the animal they told me to transform into. She was impressed, and said, "You are stronger than when we first met you. Also, nice moves, anybody facing you will go down now!" I threw back my head and laughed and said, "Yeah, anybody annoys me or my family and, I'll send them to the hospital." Kim smirked. She taught me how to transform faster, so I could move faster. I just had to keep in mind which animal I was going to transform into. But Kim taught me another way. All I had to say to transform within a second was, "Transformus (I'm going to use a ghost leopard as an example) Ghost leopard!" I do not even have to think about how the animal looks. Immensely helpful. I was not used to it, so I practised it a few times to get the hang of it. I was doing surprisingly well, but I often forgot to put 'us' after 'transform'; nevertheless, I was doing well, and now I was learning how to use my elemental powers with my shape-shifting powers. Well, this skill is useful. But wait… I had not seen my dad after the breakfast incident. After two hours of hard training, I freshened up and went to look for my father. He was not to be seen anywhere… I looked in his room, the living room, and the court. I even asked the guards, the cooks, and the ghost humans, but I got the same answer, "No, we did not see him after breakfast. He will come for lunch. Good, lunch was in fifteen minutes. I waited impatiently for lunchtime, hoping to see my dad again. Slowly, those fifteen minutes passed, and I was relieved to see him in the dining hall. I immediately asked him, "Where were you? I have been looking for you everywhere!" He ruffled my now silver hair and replied, "I was just in my office, and I do not allow anyone in. Also, I was pretty upset when you stormed off during the breakfast." I said that I was sorry and had a lot of things on my mind. Also that I could not sleep well yesterday and was annoyed when people kept asking me questions. I debated on telling him about the confrontation with the Strangers. In the end, I decided to do it anyway, I told him all about it. After I finished, he was fuming. He ran down to the Strangers room and started shouting at them for giving me nightmares and saying that I cannot take him on yet. I calmed him down and challenged my 'dad'. "So what if I cannot take you on yet, I will soon I just need a bit more time. I can take you on right now, but I just want to see if you are going to underestimate me." I used this as an excuse to ask about his moves, and he was stupid and told me all his good moves. Good advantage, I could use this against him, learn moves that he is not used to and how to block them. Wow, he does think I cannot fight, and I am just asking him. After learning all his moves, I repeated everything to Kim, the guards, and my dad, and they all agreed that they would help me learn. I am so thankful to them for helping me. Every day, I spent time with each of them, they were impressive, even Kim. I seriously had no idea an old woman could do this much!

CHAPTER 8

HOW AM I GOING TO PROVE MYSELF?

But then I remembered, I still had to fight those rats. Oh no! I was suddenly very scared because I have always been musophobic. I told this to my dad, and he said the best thing ever! "You don't have to prove yourself, you already did, and your determination to avenge your mother's death is enough for me." I was jumping with joy! Not facing rats anytime soon! Nope! Not happening! Not today, tomorrow, or anytime eventually! This is seriously the best and the most amazing news I had ever heard in my whole life. But you may be wondering, Celeste, they are just rats, what harm could they do? Well, they were not normal rats, which would just run away from me. These are dangerous rats. They have been given a strange poison, which mutated them and made them vicious. I have seen them in their cages; every time anyone used to pass their cage, they stared at us like they wanted to take a bite out of us. Their stares were bloodcurdling. I was terrified of them! I tried to avoid going through that hallway because of them. Unfortunately, my dad's office was through that hallway, so if I want to visit him, I must endure those hungry little beasts' eyes following me to the office. I seriously have no idea how my dad can even encounter that because he stays in his office the entire day and some of the house cleaners who go to clean his studio told me that there are more rats in his office. Anyways, continuing, after training, I went over to the pool, changed into my swimsuit, and floated on my back for a bit. Soon, Primrose, Camille, Mary, Kim, Sybil, Trevor, and Josh joined me along with all the kids that knew how to swim. They got in the water and the kids started splashing me! We all giggled and splashed each other; it was so much fun! When I used to live with the Strangers, I had to act very polite and posh; I could not splash, or even go in the water! The only time I could swim was during my swim lessons and all because of my old family. They had a good reputation; they thought I might 'ruin' it if I play around and do not act like a lady. I was also home-schooled but my parents let me go on my seventeenth birthday, and then I insisted that I go to school on my eighteenth birthday. If I had not gone to school, I would not have had this cool adventure. But now, I could finally splash around in the pool and not just sit on the chairs, doing nothing. We played water volleyball. I had always watched other people play it, so, I learned by looking at them and turns out, I was good at it! The fact that I knew how to play it was… incredible, I felt amazing and was proud of myself when my team (the kid's team) won against the adults. Since there were more kids than adults, we had to split out the kids' team and the two kids' teams had to take turns. My phone buzzed from where I kept it on the edge. When I found out that I could do magic, I tried things, tonnes of things and finally succeeded in charging my phone. I picked it up and it was my best friend, Bessie! Oh no! Today was her birthday, she must have called to invite me to her party! I picked it up and said hello and this is how our conversation went along:

Bessie: Hey Lysandra! How is it going? (She does not know that I am Celeste.)

Me: Great! What about you?

Bessie: It is going ok. I still miss you, how could you manage to get lost that easily in the forest?

Me: Oh, about that uh, it is a long story that I cannot… I mean do not know how to explain it.

Bessie: You always say that Lysandra, you can never explain a grandiose thing to someone.

Me: You have the same problem as well! Anyways, why did you call me? I must go soon, I am busy.

Bessie: Oh, about that, can you come to my birthday party?

Me: Um, sorry I am busy, I will not be able to make it.

Bessie: But, girl, this is going to break your streak of attending every party, sleepover, and movie night!

Me: I am busy, I cannot help it.

Bessie: Oh, come on, it is just an hour long!

Me: Girl, I told you, I am busy!

Bessie: Please with a humongous cherry on top?!

Me: Bessie, I cannot, I have loads of things to do.

Bessie: Where are you anyways, we did not see you in school for a week now!

Me: Oh uh, um, I am still in the forest. But I switched off my phone so I would have some charge left.

Bessie: How do you have internet in the middle of nowhere?

Me: About that… (I used my magic to power my phone, but she would not believe me if I said that).

Bessie: Do you want me to send you a helicopter or something to rescue you? (She is rich like me.)

Me: Nope. I am doing all right!

Bessie: But you are in the middle of nowhere!

Me: I got to go, sorry, bye! (I hang up after this.)

Bessie: Wai __________ (and the line's dead).

So, this was my conversation with Bessie who does not have an inkling about where I am, what I am doing, and who I am with, obviously. I kept the phone back and went back to my new family, they asked me who was it and I answered. They were amazed to see a phone. I do not blame them; they have never set eyes on a phone, and they were lucky they had somebody in the family who had a phone because the kids love to watch YouTube videos on it. Some of them even took pictures of themselves! Adaptive learners. I thought to myself. Dinner time was a very interactive one today! They brought out a very dusty and rusty conveyor belt. All of us were confused except, of course, my dad. He instructed me, "Use your magic to cleanse it out, then try to make it work, I want to see if you are THE Celeste Halo. If you have the power of lightning. The legendary one, I mean." I was seriously confused by now. The adults already processed everything within a few minutes and started having these confused, hopeful, and smiling faces. Nevertheless, I did as I was instructed and conducted the 'experiment' to please everyone. It turns out, I do have the lighting element. Everybody currently in the room at once bowed down and curtsied, including my dad. I was shocked and confused. I asked, "W-What is going on?" My dad had tears in his eyes. Happy tears probably because he was smiling. "You are what I thought you might be. You are THE Celeste Halo. How? Well, there is a story that I have been wanting to tell you but did not know how you would react. Anyways, here it is: When I and your mom went to war, those people (he means my parents) took you, and you got mad and flung a lightning bolt at them. That is when I knew you were still alive. Celeste Halo was a goddess who was killed by your 'parents.' Some say she died for good, and others suggested there might have been an heir to take her throne if she died. And she chose you. Also, Celeste Halo was your mother. We named you after her because you two looked so alike." I was just staring at the ceiling thinking what just happened? At last, I replied, "Huh? So, you are telling me that I am the heir of a literal goddess? I cannot believe it!" Everybody smiled and nodded. I was still staring like a fool, still trying to process everything. Kim came over and gave me a big hug. I just stood there; I shook my head and then went out of my trance. I said, "Let's just eat dinner now please, I need to get this off of my mind and I need some time to process everything." Everybody nodded and sat down at the table, I started helping myself to a bowl of vegetable soup when the Strangers came crashing into the dining hall with the ice serpent trailing along behind them, hissing with pure hatred. I asked the serpent what was wrong, and he said, "They threw a hot fire poker at me, and as you know I am made of ice, I am sensitive to fire." So, I said, "Leave them to me... uh" "Call me Icy," said the sea serpent. I replied, "Ok, Icy, leave it to me. I know how to deal with them." I at once summoned my sword using my magical power. I held it in one hand and conjured up my blue fire in the other. I sprinted after both, and after running around for a bit, I finally caught up with them. Since I already had my sword in hand, I caught hold of my 'mom' and took her hostage, I pointed my sword towards her neck and called out to my 'dad' and said, "I am going to do it if you do not QUIT bothering people I LOVE and care for. Your WIFE here is going to end up like my mother and I am going to make you watch." He begged me not to do it. Good. I made him bow down to me and said, "Remember, I told you this before, I am not scared and will not hesitate to use this deadly weapon." I said and my mom replied, "But you were so nice! You were not that mean before you met these peasants, yo—" I cut her off right then and hissed, "How dare you say that about my family?" I scratched her skin just a tiny bit, and she started screaming like a banshee. I released her and pointed out, "If you are so weak that you start crying if you get the tiniest scratch, I might as well just defeat you now. But I am going to go easy on you today just because I am hungry, and I do not feel to do it now." She started crying… more like bawling out random things about me and just one more tiny scratch had her howling in pain again. I returned to the dining hall. The guards made sure that they went back to their rooms, everybody congratulated me for the excellent job and Kim and my dad thumped me on my back and said, "Good job, kiddo. You scared them off good." I smiled and went back to drinking my vegetable soup, it had gotten cold, and so I just warmed it up a bit with my fire powers and continued drinking. I went out for a stroll after dinner with Sybil and Mary, and we just chatted about my identity. They kept asking me if I had a single inkling of doubt that I was the heir to a goddess, and I kept replying that I did not. After a solid hour of strolling around the garden, we retired to our bedrooms. They told me that my dad had given them a good-sized bedroom and that the children shared one spacious room. I decided to visit them in the morning and try to prank them by sneaking up on them and shouting boo to wake them up. I debated on doing that and I decided to just visit them and not give them a jump scare the first thing in the morning. I was super tired by the time I went into my room. All that training, chasing those… people who called MY family peasants. How dare they do it! I did not let that get to me because I wanted a good night's sleep today. I did my night routine and these are the steps I completed.

Step 1: Wash face with lukewarm water.

Step 2: Put on an Aloe-Vera face mask.

Step 3: Just chill with the face mask for thirty minutes and read a book for a while.

Step 4: Take off the mask and rinse the face with lukewarm water.

Step 5: Take a shower.

Step 6: After the shower, wash face with a face cleanser.

Step 7: Make sure I am comfortable with what I am wearing.

Step 8: Get into bed and read till I feel sleepy or read for fifteen minutes maximum.

Step 9: Before turning off the light, try to get rid of any negative thoughts I got throughout the day.

Step 10: This is the last one, believe me. Turn off the lights and have a good night's rest.

That is my night routine. I do take a bath in the morning, but I just like to take one before sleep, it helps me. Step 9 is optional at times, I just like to do it, so nothing negative is going around in my head in the morning and also to avoid nightmares. I know, it is a bit too much, but then it is worth it. Well then, good night!

The next morning

After a good night's sleep, I was feeling very fresh the next morning. So, I got up and took a shower, I still could not get over the fact that my hair was not blonde but silver. It was long, so I could not wash it myself. It was often Mary who would shampoo the kids' hair, and similarly, my hair was also treated by her. Mary's hands are so… skilled. Precise movements. I loved it when she did my hair! After showering, I went down for breakfast and asked Sybil, "Hey, good morning, Sybil, can I see your room after breakfast?" Since her mouth was full of bread, she just nodded. I picked out pancakes, berries, and apple juice. I drizzled the pancakes with a bit of maple syrup. I wanted to prank my dad today, so I transformed into a bee; the others were also with me for the prank. My dad absolutely DESPISES wild animals in the castle; even a single fly meant my dad would rage over it for HOURS. I buzzed around his ear for a bit, then hid in the chandelier to avoid being seen. After five minutes or so, I transformed back into my normal self and started laughing. He had gotten so scared! He patted me, ruffled my hair, and said, "You're quite the prankster, Celeste." I smiled and said, "I was known for my pranks. I do not like intense pranks, amazingly simple ones that will make people laugh. That is it." I said with a casual shrug. Then I went into the Strangers' room, poked my head inside, and said, "Morning, Icy! Is everything ok in here? Report to me at once if they cause any inconvenience to you, ok?" Icy nodded and said, "Yes, Princess Celeste. As you say." I smiled and patted her head. Then I turned to the Strangers, especially my adoptive father, and growled at them (including my adoptive mom), "If you cause any trouble, there will be consequences. Big and serious consequences, I am telling you." He nodded nervously; he was trying to show me that he was scared, but I am not buying it. I know he is not scared, he is just trying to put me off my guard, so when we face each other, he thinks that they have an advantage against me. Little does he know that I have been learning all the moves, including the ones he is unfamiliar with while fighting. Following that encounter, I went down to train with Kim. I mostly learn transformation and defending skills, so I let the children come along as well. Sybil had forgotten to give me a tour of their room, so I asked Kim, and she said she would take me after training. The youngsters watched in awe as I metamorphosed into different animals and practised my defending and attacking movements. My grand animal was a ghost leopard; whenever I go out onto the kingdom streets,

I always switched into this form and prowled in the woods, reporting any misbehaviour to my dad who took care of it later. Nobody feared me because they knew I was the princess and I strictly ordered them to not bow and call me princess. When they all asked why, I replied, "Because I do not like it, it makes me feel as if I am superior to you. We are all the same family so, please, this is my first and only order. Please do not refer to me as a princess or anything. Just Celeste, and no bowing down to me as well. Thank you." Everybody in the kingdom liked me because of the rule I made. Each and every one in the kingdom secretly supported me, they all wanted me to defeat the Strangers who had killed my mother and their kind, gentle and beautiful queen. When I went back to the castle, my dad told me, "Uh, there is someone who wants to meet you. He is going to ask you a question, and I hope you say no. But it is your decision. He is a prince from another kingdom." He looked as if he was crying, and I knew what that prince was going to ask me. I comforted him and replied, "I'll hear the question and decide." My dad then told me to get dressed because I was still in my training outfit with the sword in my hand. I walked down the hallway and found Mary crying on my bed. I ran over to her and asked, "What happened, Mary? Why are you crying?" Mary told me all about the prince who is coming from our ENEMY kingdom to ask me a question. I was furious! But my dress? It was beautiful! It was a red dress with specks of orange and yellow. It was my favourite element. Fire. I had to wait for about an hour when my dad sent for me saying that our guest was there. I stepped into the room, and I immediately disliked him. He looked incapable of defending himself, forget protecting others. I hid my disappointment. My dad looked a bit happy because he was in his griffin form and could smell my feeling of disappointment. He came up to me, and asked, "Celeste Halo, can I meet my parents?" I decided to prank him, I gave him an innocent look and said, "I want to put you through a test, come with me to my training area." I just wanted to see if he could defend anyone or himself for that matter. I grew a vicious tree that jumped alive the moment I commanded him. What about the prince? Well, he started running around the yard like a scared child. I rolled my eyes, and all my family was doubling over with silent laughter to see a grown man run away from something that just chases you around for fun and does not actually hurt you. I commanded the tree to stop and went over to the prince and said, "I have made up my mind. Of course…" He looked very hopeful at that, and his face fell when I said, "No. I do not even know your name! Where are you from and how do you even know me?" Then as if to make me change my mind, he said quickly, "My name is William Smith. I am from the Kingdom of Ashes (Ziraria's enemy kingdom), and I know you because you are the legendary Celeste Halo. My parents are Kevin Smith and Iris Smith," I held up a gloved hand and stopped him. "Did you just say, Kevin and Iris? Kevin Smith and Iris Smith? Are you serious now?" Now, you may ask, why am I going nuts over this small matter? That is because Kevin and Iris are the Strangers. So, that means… ugh… I absolutely cannot think properly now. I said, "You are not allowed to enter this kingdom ever again. If you DARE to step here in this castle again, you will never see your parents." He got scared at that. He did not leave at once, so I said sorry, and just as he was about to ask why was I sorry, I blasted him away to his kingdom. Time wasted on somebody who does not even make any sense. You do not come up to a person and be like, "Can I meet my parents?" I did not even know he existed! Everybody started laughing aloud when I blasted him away to his kingdom. I started laughing too, all of us went up to Kevin and Iris's room and they were trying to hide the fact that they were hoping I had allowed their son in. They asked me as casually as they could, "So? How did the meeting go with our son? Did you accept him?" I knew it! They gave it away. I smiled and said, "Of course… I did not." They looked a bit disappointed at that, but then Kevin bellowed and stepped closer to me. I held my ground as he bellowed, "WHERE IS HE? WHERE IS MY SON?" I calmly replied, "About that, I just blasted him to where he belongs, Your Kingdom of Ashes. I do not even understand what kind of name that is. Is everything made of ash there?" I mocked. They were fuming but stayed silent. Of course, they could not say anything. Is the Kingdom of Ash even real? I have been here for a couple of weeks now and I have read all the books about kingdoms, and I did not come across this kingdom! I asked them, "As a matter of fact, does your 'kingdom' even exist or it is just a myth?" They stammered, "O-of co-course i-i-it's r-real." I came back savagely at them, "Why are you stammering then, huh?" Before they could answer, I spun around on my heels and went out of the room, laughing while my family stuck their tongue out at them, and left behind me. I was about to say something to my dad when Prim (Primrose) and Camille came up to me and said, "That was impressive, Celeste! That was some savage comeback!" I thanked them, turned towards my dad, and said, "Dad, I sort of knew what that 'prince' wanted to ask me, so I planned out everything." My dad remarked to that, "How did you plan within five seconds?" I smiled and said that I had my ways. Then I made Kim take me to the rooms where they slept. I followed them and unfortunately, we had to walk through the rat's hallway. No wonder they were so reluctant to bring me here. I did not dare to look at the rats and just followed them through the hallway. When we finally reached their room, I was pleased to see that they were given an expansive room, so everybody fit in comfortably. They kept two rooms, one for the men and the other for the women. My dad even gave the kids their room, which, of course, they were more than happy to share. Good, my dad was treating them well! I spent the entire day with my family in the pool, we had our lunch there as well! We had soup, boiled chicken, and rice for lunch, and for dinner, we had soup as my dad is obsessed with soup, mashed potato, mushroom, and fish, the tastiest combination ever. For dessert, we had my favourite, Phoenix Bread.

I changed into my normal clothes and just went up to my room to relax and finish reading the book I was reading the other day. Kim lent it to me because I could not find any adventure books in the library, so I had to ask Kim to lend me one. It was about a unicorn that was stolen and fought for his life and returned as the King of all unicorns. I was currently on the part where he was stolen by the baddies of the story. I did not know why, but I had this sudden urge to go down and transform into a unicorn. So, I did exactly that, although I did not get a benefit out of it; that is what I thought because William was back. I did not how and when, but he was back. I told him not to as I changed into a firefly because I did not want to be seen. It was also a good disguise because there are a lot of fireflies at night here, so it fits perfectly. William looked around and saw nothing. In a few minutes, I changed into a ghost because fireflies are always glowing, and the hallway was dark so he might see me. I quietly followed him into Kevin and Iris's room! What does he think he is doing? Wandering around the castle! He went into the room, but I could not slip in before the door closed. After some time, I figured out that I could go through the walls, but not the doors. Weird, but sure. By the time I understood that I could go through walls, the conversation was already over. All I heard was a 'bye' and a 'see you tomorrow'. It was not worth it, but I at least knew that they are going to meet tomorrow. I have to create a plan to somehow stop him from entering the castle. I went back to my room to brainstorm a few ideas, my favourite one so far was an invisible line of electricity and fire. Mm. Sounds good. It is worth a shot anyway.

CHAPTER 9

IS MY IDEA GOING TO WORK?

I finished setting up my trap. Then went around and put up signs in each house, warning them about it. I returned to the castle and climbed back into bed, ready to sleep. I kept thinking if my defence was strong enough or not. I was cautious because I did not want to hurt the citizens, so I made a system where the people inside the city would be able to get in and out. However, outsiders would not be able to enter, and luckily, we have no visitors tomorrow. How do I know this? I might have just woken up my dad to ask him this. He was so grumpy! After a lot of grumbling and grunting, he woke up and drowsily asked me, "Do we have any visitors coming tomorrow? Why do you want to know that?" I told him the whole reason and he was mad at me for sneaking out but was also pleased with me that I found out what was going on when his back was turned. Then, he asked me, "How do you predict all of these uh… um… let's just say… troublesome situations?" My reply to his question was, "I just started to feel sick, or started to have butterflies in my stomach and have the sudden urge to do something. Today, I was reading a book about unicorns, then had the sudden urge to transform into one. So, I came downstairs, saw William, and followed him around in firefly form, then changed into a ghost, so that he would not see me in the dark hallway. He went inside Kevin and Iris's room, but I did not realize that I could not go through doors but could go through walls. By the time I figured this out, their little conversation was already over. We discussed this for some time, and then I went to Kim's bedroom and told them all about this detective work that I did. She said that they were impressed. Sometime later, I climbed up in bed, curled up with my teddy, and fell asleep. Lost in my dreams about unicorns, griffins, and all sorts of mystical animals. It was wonderful, I almost did not want to wake up in the morning because of it! But I did anyways because we were going to hang out in the pool today after my training. I was still questioning my trap in the morning. But my family reassured me that it was perfect. I told them, "As a matter of fact, he is not that hard to blast away because that boy does not even resist! Yes, you may think, 'But, you can't resist if the force is too strong!' I know, but my magic still does not have enough force yet. You can resist magic by pushing forward. It is that easy!" Kim said that this was correct and that my magic was not developed yet, so it was not that hard to push through it. I trained for a few hours, just refining my skills, and trying to conjure my magic faster, switching between each element as quickly as I could. Later, I went to the pool and got changed into my swimming costume. We had our breakfast in the pool and I was trying to make pretty designs in the water using fire, but the fire kept burning out. At last, I decided to do it in the air instead, because I was getting better at that at least. The kids watched in awe as the fire weaving through the air created reflections in the water. After some time, I figured out how to weave fire in water. It was beautiful; the kids and the adults watched in awe as fire mixed in with water, creating lukewarm water in the pool. I created a fire phoenix. We stayed in the pool for a couple of hours, then had lunch in the big garden. There were so many butterflies: pink, blue, yellow, you name it, and so many flowers as well! Daisies, roses, sunflowers and so many more. The weather was also very calm, and a soft, cool breeze passed us occasionally. After lunch, we strolled around the town, talked to everyone, and asked them how they were doing. It was so peaceful! Oh, no. I spoke too soon. Because just as I was about to say that to Josh, a riot broke out near the border of the town. We all sprinted down there and I was shocked to see William tackling a young man, and that young man was… Trevor! William kept repeating, "How do you get in? Tell me now!" I broke them apart and kept plunging my wind element into William's stomach and asked him, "What are you doing here, and how dare you hurt one of my family members?" I gave him an intense glare which he trembled under and said, "A good day to you, my dear princess." He did a gesture that was, I guess, a bow. I held him by the collar using the wind element and said, "What did I tell you about entering my kingdom again? I am sure I said that if you set foot in my territory again, you will never see your parents again. Am I right, Dad?" My dad nodded and I looked at William with coldness piercing in my eyes. He begged me not to hurt his parents, but I dragged him up to them anyways and pushed open the door. Kevin and Iris were shocked to see their son held hostage by me. Iris screamed at me, "Leave my son alone! If you hurt him, I do not know what I will do, but, definitely, I will hurt you." I replied frostily, "Well, then try me. I warned him, if he was going to step into my kingdom, there will be consequences. I wonder what I should do to punish him." I just pretended to think about his punishment to torture them, as they did to my dad. As I was heading out of the room, William tried to follow out, but I shoved him inside the room, glared at him and slammed the door hard behind me, and locked it. I could hear banging from the insides and shouts, "GET ME OUT OF HERE RIGHT THIS INSTANCE!" I did not pay any attention to that and never looked back as I went to my room. The next morning, Kevin casually stated to me, "You cannot pick a fight with me. If you do, you are going to end up like your mother. We are going to make your dad watch you fall. Again. Like he had to watch your mother fall." I was honestly so mad at this. I nearly punched him but controlled myself. I made my hands into fists, clenching them. I calmed myself down and drawled, "Oh really? Do you want to try me? I bet I could knock you down within a second." He replied, "You think so? Ok then, I challenge you to a duel between us two." My dad began to object but I cut him off mid-sentence and responded, "Sure, you're on." Everybody started looking worried. I sounded confident but, within, I felt as if I had made a big mistake. Oh well, at least it is tomorrow, I have enough time to train. Kim strolled near me and said while circling me like a shark circling a fish, "Are you sure, Celeste? I do not think you are strong enough. It is not too late to decline this proposal." I answered, "But then, I am going to sound as if I fear him. It would make me look small, also I do want to get my revenge on him. I know all his moves and how he is going to use them against me." Camille had overheard my conversation with Kim and said, "We do not want you to get hurt, though! You saved the whole village from the beasts, found that comfortable cave for us, and even saved me and my mom from Kevin and Iris!" I smiled and said that it was my pleasure. Kim told me to train and rest up, so I was energized for tomorrow's duel. The rest of my day was chill, not lying. We trained for some time, and I refined my skills and moved more like a snake, quickly and nimbly to avoid any casualties. Then, we headed over to the pool, and since it was big, I could transform into a dolphin to make the children happy. I let each of them ride on my back as I swam back and forth. Lunch was fantastic! We had fish and chips, while I taught them how to make this recipe along with a strawberry milkshake. As soon as I had finished eating, my phone buzzed. I swam over to it and picked it up. It was Bessie, again. This was our conversation. I held up a finger to my lips to hush everyone as Bessie said:

Bessie: Hi Lysandra! (I still have not told her about this adventure.)

Me: Hi Bessie, what's up?

Bessie: We are worried; we have not seen you for almost two months now! Your parents also went missing a month or so after you. Are you still in the forest? Do you need help?

Me: (Reluctantly) Um… It would be helpful if I could tell you something…

Bessie: Sure, tell me anything.

Me: So… what exactly happened when I got lost in the forest was… (I told her the story you are currently reading now.)

After I was done with my story:

Bessie: (Silent) You are not Lysandra; you are Celeste Halo?

Me: Yes. Apparently. Why are you so silent? Is everything ok?

Bessie: We are learning about that in school. So, it is true, your mother did leave an heir to take over the nature element. Oh my god, Lysandra—I mean Celeste. I cannot believe my own best friend is a mystical goddess.

Me: I know. Shocking.

Bessie: So, Celeste, defeat Kevin and Iris. They act sweet when you are around but ever since you got lost in the forest, they have been acting ever so rude to all of us. I had a feeling you were not their biological daughter. You did not act or talk like them.

Me: I suppose you were right. Yes, I never did act like them.

Bessie: Also, can you send me a picture of your new hair?

Me: Sure, I do not see the harm in it.

Bessie: Ok, bye. I will be awaiting your picture.

Me: Ok. Bye.

We hung up and I took a picture of my new hair and sent it. Bessie immediately replied:

Oh my god! Your hair is beautiful! You could style your hair in a braided bun! It would suit you in your training leathers.

I replied:

Ok, thanks, I will try it, I think it will look cute too. I still cannot believe I have silver hair! Ok, I got to go now. Bye!

And with that, I went offline.

I put my phone down and turned to talk to everyone. The younger kids kept asking what I just clicked on my phone, and I replied that I took a picture of myself and offered to take one of them as well. They immediately said yes. They were excited to have a picture taken of them but then were disappointed because it was not much except for a flash of light. I showed them the picture I just took and they were surprised to see it captured and not moving. I explained that pictures do not move. It is like being paused in time. After dinner, I went up to bed earlier than usual so that I was well rested. The duel was going to be in the morning before breakfast, so I also made sure that I ate properly at dinner.

After doing my night routine, I fell asleep. I had good dreams and no nightmares as I far as I can remember.

CHAPTER 10

THE DUEL

And guess what? It is daybreak already! I woke up prematurely than usual, freshened up, and went down to my exercise yard to stretch and cram in some last-minute practice. A few hours later, Kevin and Iris came down with William from their rooms (where they are locked up the entire day; we slide in their breakfast, lunch, and dinner through a pet door) into our duelling area. I had about two advantages. First, I knew all the movements AGAINST Kevin's. Second, I have magic-based capabilities, but Kevin, Iris, and William do not. Kevin smirked at me; everybody took a seat, while I went down to the duelling ground to face Kevin. Everybody was arguing over who would win. The adults were sceptical while the kids argued with William about who would triumph. We bowed to each other and stepped away about four to five steps. He gave me a cold stare, which I mocked with an eye roll. My dad nervously announced, "Ok, if Celeste wins, Kevin and Iris must do what she orders you for a year; the same applies if

Kevin wins. You may start." At that command, I shot out a burst of lighting when Iris screamed, "She has lightning powers? But that's not fair, Kevin does not have powers!" My dad replied to that as coldly as he could despite keeping an eye on me, "I am the monarch, and I never said that she couldn't use her powers, did I?" I was busy fighting. However, I still heard everything. I shifted into a ghost leopard and lunged at him, but he swerved, then he drew up the blade behind me, but I was spontaneous to change into a phoenix and fly away, then I swooped down and pecked his eye. Blood started pouring out, blinding him for life. After five minutes of him running away from me and me chasing him around in a phoenix or ghost leopard form, he lunged at me to try to hurt me in some way, but I switched to my most powerful form, the sabretooth tiger. I ran after him; he looked scared but still lunged left and right. He finally cried out, "OK, STOP! You win! I give up!" After five minutes of me chasing him as a sabretooth tiger, I shifted back and grinned, "Advised you that I would be victorious. All you did was to underrate me." He looked a bit introverted and angry. I smiled as everyone looked relieved that I had escaped without a single scratch on me. I recalled my prize and said, "You can start by cleansing up the garden and watering the flowers. If you mess that up, I'll make sure that you have a big penalty, and I know precisely what to do." They angrily got to work, and I assigned Icy to watch over them if they caused any disturbance. Everybody calmed down and we made our way over to our pool. Sybil said to me, "Oh my god! Are you ok? That was fantastic! Excellent job, kiddo." She patted me on the head, and I smiled. A few minutes later, Icy slithered towards me, hissing, and said, "They're creating issues, they squashed all your favourite flowers." I was furious! How dare they? Oh well, time for their punishment. I did warn them about messing up this straightforward job of just watering the plants. I quickly dried myself up and switched to my usual clothes, then stormed down to where I had left them to water the plants. The once gorgeous garden was now decimated into a bunch of trampled and crushed flowers and bushes. I walked a little further and the only thing I saw was the Smith family laughing like maniacs, stating, "Ha! We captured little Icy and trampled on her favourite flowers!" I was perplexed. If they caught Icy, how did she manage to escape and tell me the news? I asked her how she managed to do that, and the sea ice serpent replied, "Oh, about that, my kind of serpent can go through anything, we aren't exactly ghosts, but we can go through things, it's a bit hard to explain, but I'm sure you get it." I nodded and asked, "What do we do about them now?" Icy and I thought for a moment, and then an idea abruptly struck me. I whispered to Icy, "I know! Try to scare them somehow and I will do the rest." The serpent gazed at me with inquisitiveness and nodded, but before she moved away, I asked her, "Do you have any kind of, I do not know... a device that can show me as a ghost, maybe? That would be terrifying and cool." Icy thought for more than a minute, she looked deep in thought and then asked, "Do you have a cauldron and... what is your favourite colour? Oh yes, light purple. Do you have some by any chance? I need the dye… I also need a… let us see… ah ha! A necklace." I thought for a moment then replied more to myself than Icy, "Hmm, I think I might have the… purple dye, necklace, not sure about the cauldron, we could ask the chefs about it… I have most of the things. I know that you are going to make a potion to make me appear as a ghost because if I change into a ghost-human, they cannot see me… You are brilliant, Icy! Come on! We must run…" As I turned around to stand up, Kevin, Iris, and William looked at us, grinning. Kevin said to me, "Well, well, well. Look who it is, is our little girl devising a plan?" I glared at him and said, "Oh, please. Mind your own business. Did I ask you to intervene in my business? Did I even ask for your opinion about what I am doing? William, keep your long nose out of this." Iris shrieked me, "DON'T YOU DARE SPEAK TO MY SON LIKE THAT!" Then she stomped out of the garden and I called out to them, "Who do you think is going to clean us this mess you made, huh?" They completely ignored me and went up to their room. Ugh! They are so annoying! I scowled at their back. Oh, I was going to get them someday… Wait… I was going to avenge my mother… YES! We could use the prank… let me see… my dad told me I looked like a younger version of her… I have the perfect idea for it. That is the way I was looking for to get back at them! Icy went back to the pool and relaxed the entire day while I grew the trampled flowers. There, good as new, as if nothing ever happened. We executed the plan. I just hope they did not hear most of it, if they did, my plan would not work effectively. For a couple of days, I helped Icy make the magic necklace, and oh boy, it was EXTREMELY complicated, but it seemed easy to Icy, and she did it with ease. I followed along, bringing all the ingredients she needed. After we set up the necklace, all of us sat down to plan out the prank (my ghost-human family as well). Kim said to me, "Are you sure about this? From what you told us, it seems like they already might know what you are doing." I reassured her by saying, "Don't worry, I'll make a backup plan if needed." Sybil opened her mouth to say something but bit her lip and closed her mouth. We continued working on the plan. That night, I went to bed a bit full of ideas and happiness because I won the duel without even a tiny scratch. I fell asleep, smiling and thinking about the prank, I was known in my school for my pranks too.

CHAPTER 11

THE PRANK

As the sun was on the horizon, I got up, raced downstairs, and was surprised to see Icy already awake and adding the last-minute changes to the fantastic prank. I was seriously beginning to question the idea because the Smiths had heard everything we had planned. Icy reassured me that even if they did hear about our plan, they would've no idea because she told me the time was incorrect. She had said that the time was 5:10 pm. But it was 10:05 or somewhere approximately. I replied, "You are a genius, Icy! You had a backup plan and everything!" She looked at me proudly but humbly, and replied, "Thanks, it was your idea in the first place. If you had not thought about a device that could show you as a spirit, I would not have considered this fantastic idea." I smiled and said, "Can't wait to get this prank up and running." It was 8:00 am. Another two hours, but it was breakfast time! I wanted to keep my energy level as elevated as I could. Icy warned me during breakfast that the necklace quickly runs out of the potion. So, if you refill it with the potion, it takes about a minute or two to recharge. It works for fifteen minutes. Oh well, that should be long enough to deliver my statement. I formed a plan about what I wanted to say, and finally (about two pages later), I figured out what I wanted to say. I looked at the ancient clock, and it was 8:15! That meant it was breakfast time! When I arrived at the table, there was my favourite dish: Spinach-Mushroom Strata. Swiss cheese that melts in your mouth and buttery mushrooms sautéed with fresh thyme make this savoury, earthy spinach strata. Also, my other favourite is shirred eggs with leeks. I gasped because the first time I had this was when I had just revealed myself to my actual dad and we moved into this gorgeous chateau. My dad beamed, ruffled my hair, and said, "Like it? The chefs made your favourite dishes today because you did well in the duel yesterday!" I smiled and greeted everyone with a "Good morning" and all of us took a seat. Kim sat beside me and asked, "So, how is the plan going?" I responded, "Pretty good, we're going to carry it out at 10:05 approximately." Sybil answered, "That is specific. But I remember you telling us that the Smiths had already heard the conversation… So, if they already know about the trick, they might be ready." I smiled and looked at Icy who was currently busy devouring a bowl of scrambled eggs (she does not like shirred). She looked up with a look of innocence and I started giggling; she gave me a perplexed look, and I clarified as to why I was laughing, "You have egg all over your whiskers, Icy! Oh my god, I never knew you were so messy!" She gave me a timorous look and I gently wiped the eggs with my napkin. Half an hour later, all of us got up. We still had time to conduct the prank so, I went around town, greeting everyone. A few minutes later, I saw a riot had broken out again. I darted over to the edge of the kingdom, and there was Ziraria's fire dragon guard alongside a hybrid who could turn into a phoenix and Pegasus against the Kingdom of Ashes' water demon and a fire hydra. It seemed as if Ziraria was winning this tough battle. I joined them in my ghost leopard form and lunged left to right, attacking wherever I could. I was careful to not attack Ziraria's dragon and the hybrid. A good ten to fifteen minutes later, the enemies finally backed off and headed straight to their kingdom, scared. By then, a huge crowd had also gathered around the place we were battling against the demon and hydra. I petted the dragon and the hybrid when I changed back into my human form. I could also see the Halos (yes, the village ghost humans are part of the Halo family now) pushing through the crowd with apprehensive looks on their faces. Camille and Primrose started fussing over the dragon, hybrid, and me, searching for any cuts or injuries. I kept telling them that I was fine. Abruptly, Icy darted towards me and said, "It is time! Come on! We agreed on 10:05. It is 10:15 now!" I just stared at her, flabbergasted and wide-eyed, then cried, "OH NO! OK, come on let us go!" Before anyone could say anything, Icy slithered and I sprinted towards the castle, leaving the townspeople perplexed and my family worried. It was 10:20 by the time we got everything set up. I exclaimed, "Where's the potion that we were going to use to refill this necklace?" Icy scrambled around, trying to find it in vain. I was panicking by now, suddenly Kim came up to me and said, "Are you looking for this? I think Icy might have dropped it when she was rushing over to you." Icy thanked Kim repeatedly. Sybil strolled over to me and casually told me, "This is missing something… what is your favourite… flower? I told her that my favourite flowers were a Sterling Silver Rose. Sybil quickly asked me to grow her one and within a minute, she had crushed the flowers and mixed it up together. Then told me, "There." I thanked her and we started on the prank. Or at least we tried to. Turns out, the Smiths had been eavesdropping on our business, AGAIN! We turned around and saw three pairs of feet running towards the Smith's bedroom. The only people who were allowed to go were the house cleaners who gave them food every day. So, they heard our plan again. This was going to be a big failure. Oh well, it was worth a shot. I wore the beautiful moonstone pendant that my dad gifted me, which also was my mother's favourite piece of jewellery, as I was told. Fingers crossed, this idea is going to work. Before I could transform, Icy warned me, "Be careful, ok? You can go through everything; people hear you and see you. You only have fifteen or twenty minutes to say whatever you want. Then, you will be a normal ghost-human, but you must be invisible because the human ghost enchantment was only made for this generation of the village people and no outsider is supposed to or can have this form even if he or she had transforming powers. That is way too overpowered."

I nodded and said, "That is a lot of information, but I got it. I can go through anything, people hear me and see me, and my time limit is fifteen to twenty minutes… I will change back into a normal ghost-human… got it. Noted." I went ahead and transformed into the ghost and went into the room. I knew it. They were ready for it and were not scared, Kevin said to me, "Did our little princess try to scare us with that trick? It did not work now, did it? I know it is such a disappointment." William and Iris shook with silent laughter. I decided to give it all that I got, and said in a very royal voice to try to imitate what my mom would sound like if she were alive, "Did you just call me a princess? Did you forget who I am? I am Celeste's mother." Everyone tensed up. It was a long and awkward silence, and it was broken by Iris who stuttered, "You mean my best friend, Celeste?" I nodded and replied, "You got it right, good job." I clapped sarcastically and said, "Turning to the more important points. I saw you, while I was doing my daily checking rounds around the castle…" Kevin interrupted, "But you're dead, how can you do your daily rounds?" I laughed and replied, "About that, I can go down to Earth whenever I want and I go down in the morning, afternoon, evening and sometimes if I cannot get any sleep, at night. Anyways, turning to the subject of this discussion, I saw you while I was doing my morning rounds that you had ruined my child's favourite flowers, I was honestly so disappointed…" William interrupted my speech AGAIN. It is disgusting that I cannot even finish one sentence and he always interrupts! Here is how it went, "But…" William interrupted, but I cut him off and said sharply, "Do not interrupt me, you are in my territory so that means you have to listen to me more than you interrupt." I started again, sweetly this time, "I request to not do that anymore, or I shall have to pay you another visit, which, next time will be more serious and harsher than the first encounter. My time is up, but remember, I am watching you. Good day to you." I gave a curtsy, transformed into an invisible ghost-human, and flew out of there. As soon as I got out of that room, I changed into my most prized animal, a ghost leopard and sprinted all the way to the training yard. Me, Icy, and all the Halos had agreed to meet up near my training yard so that we could share how it went without anyone prying because the entrance had a series of passcodes that only the Royal family knew. I told them all about my encounter and they were surprised because even if they had heard most of our plan, they still fell for it. Dad asked me to do Mum's voice again, and when I did it, he said it sounded exactly like her, so maybe that is why they got scared.

CHAPTER 12

THE EARTHQUAKE

As soon as I finished telling them the story and getting all those comments, the ground suddenly shook, the force was so strong that all of us were knocked out of our feet and the whole town was a wreck within seconds. All the houses had crumbled down, windows were smashed into smithereens, parks and my personal garden were ruined, and all paths had a big crack straight down the middle. It was total chaos, people running around, trying to gather their valuable stuff, their kids, pets, and everything they could grab while escaping their houses and everything that was important to them. The only evacuation area was my training yard, it was open for emergencies like this; people flooded in, and kids were trying to keep up, but unfortunately, some of them got separated from their families. Those lost kids came to us, and once peace was restored, the kids could find their families. I transformed into a jackrabbit and hopped around, looking at the destruction. It had a magnitude of at least 5.5 on the Richter scale, looking at all the damage and chaos. I quickly made sure there was nothing trapped underneath the house in the rubble. But as I came across the last street in the town and my favourite street, Hazelnut St, I saw a poor squirrel and a marsh tit stuck under a tree.

I love Hazelnut St because it has tonnes of parks with loads of wildlife, flowers and so much more to see. Ok, back to the story.

I immediately called the Halos and asked them to help me. They agreed, they tried to lift the tree; it was too heavy for them so they couldn't lift it, so I used my wind powers to lift it while they picked up the animals. Turns out they were only babies, which meant, they still had a long journey to go through. We went back to the evacuation area, and I healed the animals the best I could. They were looking all right but the bird could not fly, so I just bandaged the wing up a bit and made them a nest out of flowers so that they could rest, and the squirrel went up and snuggled up beside the marsh tit! It was adorable! While they were sleeping, we looked around the damages that happened to the town; it would take months, even years to rebuild the town. The parks would be easy, I can grow them with my magic, the castle was mostly untouched, except for a few pillars here and there that had come apart. That would be easy to fix, we just needed cement, I guess. I declared when I finished planning everything out, "I suppose we could all camp out in the castle, there is food, water, warmth and all the necessities that we could possibly need. The children could sleep in my room, there are separate rooms for men and women which I think is perfect, we just have to add a couple more beds… There is a shower as well… I think, I am quite sure, I can make all the items we need to rebuild the town with my powers… Yep, that is all from me. Any question? No? So, let us get on with the plan!" The architects of the town told me that they already had a big stock of powdered cement, but they did not have water yet because the earthquake broke all the water pipes. I asked them to bring it to me and used my water element to prepare the cement mixture. Next, we started repairing the pillars to make sure that no casualties occurred. All of us were busy when I suddenly realized that Kevin, Iris, and William were still inside the castle. I asked Mary and she said, "Wait, so you are telling me that the Smiths are still inside?" Her eyes grew wide with horror, and she rushed to tell everyone the shocking news. The men were mostly just neutral, replying with just an "Ok," but the women grew restless, and when I announced that I would go look for them, they all said that they wanted to come with me as well. We wandered around the castle, hmm, the castle was strong! Except for a couple of broken pillars here and there, there was not a single crack that I could notice. I was walking at the back of the group and was just admiring the castle's strength when Sybil let out a piercing scream, I rushed forward and gasped in horror. The Smiths were under a pillar, and they seemed to have passed out, Sybil's scream made everyone run in our direction. Trevor and Josh came running and there was this very awkward silence. It was Trevor who broke the silence he asked me, "What on earth happened here? Is everyone ok? Why did Sybil scream?" I was transfixed and rooted on the spot, staring at the Smiths. I pointed at them very slowly and stuttered, "T-That h-h-happened…" Kim shook me real hard and said, "Snap out of it, and help them!" I shook myself and lifted the pillar with my wind element while Mary pulled out Iris, Trevor pulled out Kevin, and Josh pulled out William. I dropped the pillar on the grass and inspected their injuries, some of them were severe, while others were just cuts and bruises. I said to myself, "Mm, the cuts and bruises will be easy to heal, but the severe ones will take a long time. I will need the first aid kit, which should be in my room. We are going to have to find some ointment to soothe the pain and prevent infections… Ok! I know what to do." I rushed about, gathering the materials I would need for the procedure. I set off healing them one by one, starting with the small injuries, and then moving on to the bigger and more complex ones. Sybil, Mary, and Kim helped me while the kids ran about emptying the water bowl used to clean up the blood and the men set about fixing the pillars of the castle. About half an hour later, I and the ladies were done dressing their wounds. Primrose and Camille were making a medicine to revive them. Mary forced a bit through their clamped mouths and within seconds, they were awake. They looked around, dazed, and asked, "What's going on?" I looked at them and said, "When the earthquake struck, I suppose you were trying to get out, but then one of the pillars fell on you then all of you fell unconscious. We revived you and that is exactly what happened." The Smiths looked at us in confusion and Iris asked me, "But we did so many things to annoy you. Despite that, you and your family bothered to help us and took the effort to make the difficult potion. Why?" I looked at Kim and she shrugged and said, "It was Celeste's idea in the first place. If she hadn't noticed that you were missing, we would have never even remembered. If it were not for her, we would not have the ability to drag you out from underneath the pillar to help you. So, the person you should be saying thank you to is your 'daughter,' whom you illegally kidnapped from the king, and killed her mother despite you being in their territory. They were so kind, yet you had the audacity to do all these, but Celeste still helped you. She is the one you should be saying thank you to, not us. If she had not even bothered, we would not have bothered to ever be here right now." I cut her off saying, "Whoa, whoa, whoa, calm down Kim. That is a trifle too harsh, you know what I mean? Go easy on them. I know they do annoy me a bit, but they might have learnt their lesson now and we can organize an alliance ceremony and Dad can be friends with them like he was nineteen years ago! Just go easy on them. Ok?" I gave them a little smile, Sybil argued, "But, Celeste, Kim is right. They did do a lot of bad things. I mean I am not saying that they can't say thank you to you, they can. They should. But we must be hard on them." I cut her off by holding one of my hands up, motioning her to stop. "Come with me, we are making lunch now, join us." William replied, "But everybody is going to hate us if we step in with you." I waved him off and said, "Tsk. Tsk. You are going to go there with the princess of Ziraria. If anybody dares make fun of you, they can't, because I'm with you. I can tell them to stop whenever I want." They cautiously said ok and followed me to my training yard where everyone was relaxing or cooking lunch. The pillars were almost done (except for the ones at the back). Everybody present in the yard stared at the Smiths, wondering what they were doing, walking behind their princess. I kept my head high and shoulders back while the Smiths kept theirs down as we walked through the crowd and eventually got to where all the Halos would be sitting for lunch. My dad stared at them and finally asked me, his anger rising per word, "What are they doing here?" I soothed him and said, "Hey, hey, hey, it's all right. They said that they were sorry; also, if anything goes wrong, I'll manage it." He calmed down and told me, "Ok, I will give them three tries, if you can oversee all of them and they learn their lesson, I will not do anything, but if they do not listen to you, I will take care of them." I calmed him down and said that I can and will manage any mischief they cause. Anyways, lunch was impressive! Salad, grilled fish, and mashed potato, and of course, my favourite, Phoenix Bread. Dad maintained eye contact with Kevin during lunch. I noticed Primrose shot nervous looks; her eyes darting between Kevin and King Louis or Lunarquills. I tried hard to ease them out. After lunch, the kids had an afternoon nap while the others worked on the pillars. By evening, we had set up everything in the castle to ensure everybody had a good night's rest. After resting, we would get on with rebuilding the town.

A few months later

A few months later, we are finally done! That took ages! It was seriously a big team effort, and I was glad to see Dad and Kevin becoming friends again. Both started hanging out with each other, talking to each other about their kingdoms. I also learned that the reason I could not find a book about the Ash Kingdom was because my dad had burned it as he thought IF I returned, I would not read the enemy kingdom's book. But now, the two kingdoms are not in rivalry anymore; they are planning to have alliances. The ceremony is going to take place on my twentieth birthday, which is also the time I will be becoming Queen. Eek! I am so excited! We were currently in… 9th of November, which means I still have a long time to go till my birthday; my birthday is on 13 January. Since we were done rebuilding our town, I invited all the town kids and my siblings to join me in the pool to play or something. The kids looked extremely excited, but their parents were reluctant. I assured them that I do not mind taking care of the children while all the adults relax after those hard months of building. The parents said that they were grateful to me and would do anything to help me. I thanked them and made my way to the pool with the kids, partly because I did not want to go to the pool all alone, and partly because I wanted all the adults to have a break from taking care of their kids. Everyone splashed around the pool. I taught the kids the front crawl, backstroke, and pencil jump. The youngsters looked at me with fascination as I demonstrated each of them in detail. I made a couple of older kids try the tricks and… SUCCESS! They are quick learners! Although they were a bit scared doing the pencil jump, they still did impressively. I just had to hold both of their hands and all they had to do was jump into the water. We had fun until lunchtime and then dried up and had lunch. Since the town was fixed, everyone could go back to their houses. I went up to my room and read my favourite book, *The Unicorn King*. It was a fascinating book. As soon as I settled in, the Halo kids came in and begged me to read them the story that I was currently reading. I read them a few chapters, and a couple of the young ones fell asleep on my pillow, between the legs of my giant teddy bear. I smiled at them and laid a few blankets over the kids so that they were warm while they slept. While I was laying a blanket over a kid who was sleeping on my huge bear, she fidgeted a bit. I paused but then realized that she only wanted to get more comfortable. I turned off the lights and made my way down. When I arrived in the courtroom, I was surprised to see Kim, Primrose, and Camille talking to Iris and William while Trevor and Josh were gossiping with Kevin. I went over to my throne beside my dad's chair, where he was currently seated. As I sat down, he told me, "Thank you, Celeste, it was really because of you. If you had not bothered to save them, we would not have ended our rivalry, we would not have become an ally, and we would not have become the friends we were nineteen years ago. Thank you, Celeste, you really do deserve to be Queen. I had a talk with all the townspeople, and they all agreed to let you be Queen because you are so kind, helpful, caring, funny, energetic, always make good decisions, help your enemies and so much more. But there is a catch, you must wait till your twentieth birthday!" I laughed and said, "Of course, I know I must wait till I am twenty years old! Anyways, I am grateful to all the people who said wonderful things about me. I also know that I might get criticism when I am Queen, but I promise I will not take it personally; instead, I will use it as a learning experience to make myself better while I am ruling the town. I also hope that none of the kingdoms have a fight. I want to keep things chill."

My dad smiled at me and said, "That is my girl! I know you will make a good Queen. I have a surprise for you. Remember the first day you came here? (I nodded.) You asked me why I looked so young? (I nodded again.) And I said that you just had to wait till we were familiarized with each other? (I nodded again.) Well, the secret/surprise is that, when I was made King, they gave me a blessing that I would live forever and would stop growing when I was about 25 years old. I made a special request to make it applicable to you as well. But there is another side to it. You are mortal to stabbings and poison. Because your mother also had that blessing, but…" I quickly replied, "I know what happened to her, you do not have to explain it to me. Anyways, I will go check on the kids. Be right back." With that, I got off my seat and made my way towards my room where the kids were sleeping. Most of the kids that woke up were the older ones. I did not have the heart to wake up the younger ones, so I let them sleep while the others played with some of the trinkets that I allowed them to touch. One of the kids asked me, "Whose scarf are you wearing, sissy?" I told them that

I was wearing my mum's scarf and they asked me if they could wear it for some time. I did not have the heart to say no, but I also did not trust them. Apart from the necklace that I used for the prank, the scarf was the only thing I had left as a memory of my mother, and I did not want anything to happen to it. I reluctantly said yes and gave it to them. To my surprise, they were incredibly careful with it and handed it back to me after twenty minutes. I smiled and said, "Come on, let's go down to the yard, I might be able to make you a snow slide for you to slide on. It is winter anyways, so I don't think it will melt."

Ok. So, taking a break from the story, we are going to do a tiny time lapse here to show you the day of my birthday. Back to the story now.

We had a good November and December… until it was my birthday! I am twenty years old and ready to be queen. But the ceremony I am looking most forward to is the alliance one. It is going to be so exciting! Anyways, the alliance party was fine. But the trouble started when I was taking the live-forever blessing. What happened was that it was not working! The priest got the wrong spell; turns out, he had lost it! Everyone scrambled around trying to find it, it was Icy who found it at last. It fell in a bed of roses when the priest was rushing to get here. Some parts of it had ripped because of the rose's thorns, but luckily, the priest knew the part where it was ripped by heart. It sure was very chaotic, but in the end, we got through the ceremony smoothly. I was finally crowned Queen of Ziraria, and my title changed from Princess to Queen Celeste. I was also crowned the Warrior Queen Celeste. The. Best. Day. Of. My. Life! I visited Village Lysandra (it was still ruined) and went back to my home, where I was called Lysandra. It felt so good to see Bessie again! We gossiped for about an hour when my guard announced that it was time for me to go. I said bye to her and added that I would be coming back to visit every day. I visited her every day if I did not have chores to do or babysit the kids. I could see my old friends, teachers, and neighbours. Everyone greeted me with a smile and good morning. Some of them even threw a returning party for me! Everything was going well, I kept training harder each day because everything was unpredictable. There could be a war between the kingdoms unexpectedly. But there was none; we were on good terms with everyone. Our town is flourishing with trade requests almost every day for rice, coffee etc. Our farms were doing fantastic! Growing fresh, juicy fruits and vegetables. Our parks were getting visitors often, everything was going great! The townspeople also wanted me as their queen, so we did not have any problems. We do have frequent floods, but that is not a big issue, considering I have water powers, so I could just suck up the water, easy enough for me. Fortunately, we did not have any more devastating disasters like the earthquake, so I am quite pleased. Kevin and my dad are like best friends now and Primrose is good friends with Iris. So, here I am, sitting in my castle, telling you, my story.

Phew, I had an extremely long journey, but I made a lot of friends, who eventually became a part of my family, made two rival kingdoms allies, and found out I had magical powers. My bone-chilling, hair-raising adventures ended. I was known as Lysandra at the beginning of the story, but now I am known as the Warrior Queen Celeste at the end. I must give credit to the people from Village Lysandra. If they had not found me, I would have been dead by now. "You have thanked us enough, Celeste. Thank yourself too, it was you who made two enemy kingdoms friends again." That is what Kim just said to me. I have so many responsibilities now which I will perform with pleasure. This has been an excessively big learning experience for me.

Thank you to all the readers as well, who took their time to read my adventures! I hope to see you another time.

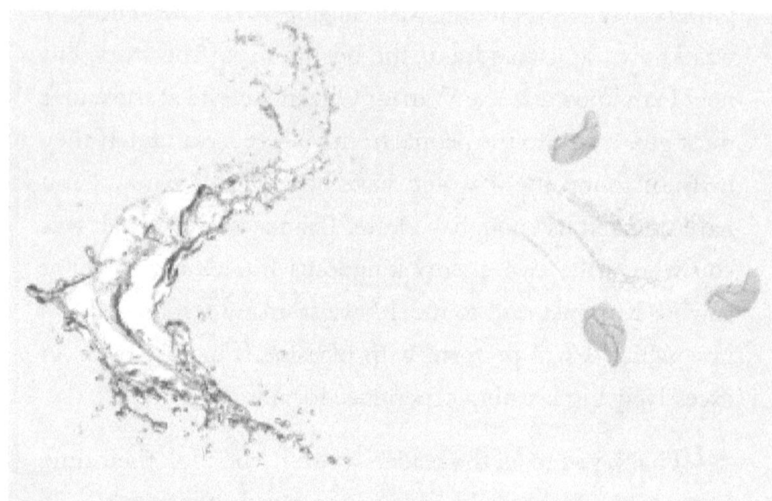

The End